D0443424

TERRITORIAL ROUGH RIDER

TERRITORIAL ROUGH RIDER

A Western Story

TIM CHAMPLIN

Five Star • Waterville, Maine

First Edition
First Printing: November 2004

Published in 2004 in conjunction with Golden West Literary Agency.

Set in 11 pt. Plantin by Liana M. Walker.

Printed in the United States on permanent paper.

Library of Congress Cataloging-in-Publication Data

Champlin, Tim, 1937–
    Territorial rough rider : a western story / by Tim Champlin.
    —1st ed.
        p. cm.
    ISBN 1-59414-010-3 (hc : alk. paper)
    1. Spanish-American War, 1898—Fiction.
    2. Coins—Collectors and collecting—Fiction.
    3. Arizona—Fiction. I. Title.
    PS3553.H265T47 2004
    813'.54—dc22   2004057982

For Dr. Rick Romfh
whose expertise and meticulous editing
greatly improved this book

Prologue

April 17, 1898
St. Louis, Missouri

Peter Ormond caught his breath at the sound of footsteps on the stairs. Heart pounding, he swung the oil painting back over the wall safe and ducked into a hall closet, pulling the door nearly closed. He recognized the heavy tread of Millard Johnson, his father's colored manservant. Johnson strode past the closet, turned into the master bedroom, and emerged a minute later. As the servant passed the crack in the closet door, Peter Ormond saw him carrying the elder Ormond's silk smoking jacket—a sure sign his father's birthday party in the library below was winding down. The old man always affected a smoking jacket to ape the British elite, even when he was in the house alone. As far as those at the party knew, Peter Ormond had excused himself a half hour ago because of fatigue, and retired to his second floor room for the night.

The sound of Johnson's footsteps faded, and Peter Ormond hurried out of the closet and back to the wall safe. He had to be quick. From the stirrings and the tenor of voices drifting up as the library door was opened, he knew the guests were collecting their coats and their wives, preparing to depart. Anyone leaving the library could look up and see him standing behind the balustrade on the second floor, overlooking the entrance hall.

Peter Ormond fumbled with the combination lock, missed his mark, cursed softly, and started over. He suspected the wine was affecting his concentration and dexterity. He couldn't remember the combination, but his father never erased the numbers penciled on the bottom of the white marble base of a lamp in the master bedroom—two full left turns to seven, one full turn right to thirteen, one and a quarter turn left to twenty-four. He held his breath and turned the handle. The lock *clicked* softly, and the circular door swung open. Sweating profusely, he quickly snatched the velvet bag that held the collection of thirty-six gold coins, mounted in six, thin mahogany strips. Without opening the bag, he shoved it into the side pocket of his jacket, closed the door, and spun the dial. Then he wiped the dial and the handle and the front of the safe with his handkerchief, in order to frustrate any police who might be using this new art of fingerprint detection.

The voices below grew louder. Peter Ormond had barely time to swing the framed oil portrait back into place and drop to the floor before his father and four male guests walked into the entrance hall. Partially screened from sight by the banister, he dared not move, fearing the light from the gas chandelier would reveal his presence. He was almost sure they could hear him breathing, or his heart beating. But the men in evening clothes were merely thanking their host and saying their good byes and calling for their carriages. Peter Ormond wiggled back from the banister to lie against the wall. He heard his mother, two sisters, and four other women coming from the parlor. The visitors began donning their wraps as they prepared to leave.

It seemed an age before the voices receded. Peter Ormond ventured a peek between the spindles of the banister. Millard Johnson was holding the door for the departing company. For a few seconds, everyone's back was to him. He darted in a crouch toward the entrance to the back stairs, thirty feet away—his soft shoes noiseless on the carpet—and vanished into the darkened stairwell. No one had seen him. He half slid downward, supporting himself with stiff arms on the two hand rails, his feet touching every third or fourth step. Pausing at the bottom, he peeked carefully around the door casing into the kitchen. The cooks hired for the evening were rattling pans in the deep sink, their backs to him. He shot across the doorway and into the alcove that led to the back porch. Ten seconds later he was across the yard and slipping through the gate in the brick wall to the alley beyond. Even in darkness, he was familiar with this territory. As a child, he'd spent many a day playing up and down this alley, ranging several blocks beyond the Ormond mansion. His feet flew over the hard ruts as he sprinted toward the next street. He didn't slow down until he'd gone four blocks at a dead run. Then he heard the *clopping* of approaching horses, and ducked behind a hedge. A carriage rolled past and he emerged, knees shaking, breath coming in labored gasps. The wine and fear had given him a false energy that was quickly ebbing away. He walked three more blocks to a main thoroughfare where foot and vehicle traffic still flowed, even an hour before midnight. Ten minutes later, he managed to hail a passing cab.

"Union Station!" he yelled to the driver, yanking open the door and springing inside. In spite of the chill night, he was perspiring under his shirt and corduroy jacket as he leaned back in the hard seat. His throat was dry, and he was exhausted, but still tingled with excitement. Every sense was alert. Living on the edge of danger made him feel alive. Too bad he had moral qualms about a life of stealing, or he might even take up the outlaw trail. For thrills, it beat his present postal clerk's job, hands down. He took a deep breath to steady his wildly beating heart as the iron-shod wheels ground over the cobblestones toward the depot in the heart of the city.

Chapter One

The wine caused it. At least that's what Peter Ormond wanted to believe. That extra glass of pale, dry sherry had tipped the balance of his good judgment and provided the reckless courage to plunder his father's wall safe and make off with a set of rare gold coins valued at $50,000.

Two hours later, when he was seated in a Kansas-bound railroad car with the coins deep in his pocket, Ormond sobered up enough to realize what he'd done. Chill April air, tainted with coal smoke, seeped in around the ill-fitting coach windows, and he huddled in his jacket, shivering. The deed was done; there was no turning back. He was certain his father, Cornelius Edwin "C.E." Ormond, had discovered the coins missing by now, and would be raving mad, notifying the police.

Since Ormond had the combination, he'd pulled off the theft with no noise or physical damage to the safe, thereby making himself an immediate suspect. But why had he made such a stupid mistake? Had it been only a few hours ago? It seemed like last week.

Ormond had returned from Prescott, Arizona Territory, to celebrate C.E.'s sixtieth birthday. He never called his fa-

11

ther "Dad" or "Father". The old man had always been just
C.E. to him and everyone who knew him, except for Ormond's mother who never called him anything but Edwin.
Peter Ormond and his father had never been close, but that
was no reason to steal from the old man, although the loss
of even these valuable coins would cause little financial distress. More likely, it would hurt C.E.'s pride, and Ormond
realized that's what he'd meant to do—to bring down the
old man a peg or two, to deflate his cockiness and embarrass him in front of his friends.

Normally he wouldn't have considered such a thing. It
was a desperate, spur-of-the-moment act. No, on reflection,
he decided, it wasn't impromptu at all. It was the culmina-
tion of years of demeaning remarks and put-downs by an
arrogant, overbearing, authoritative parent whose lifetime
habit continued, even after his son had grown and left
home. C.E. never failed to belittle Peter Ormond in front of
friends or guests, or even strangers, by commenting on how
he wished he had a son worthy of carrying on his name. He
always grinned when he said it, but there was no humor. "If
Peter would only get off his lazy butt and make something
of himself . . . ," and so on. Like others before, the birthday
guests this evening had smiled nervously, looking from father to son, assuming this was some sort of long-standing
family joke.

But he knew better. This was C.E.'s way of saying his
son would never be a success, no matter what he did with
his life. "Never amount to a hill of beans . . . ," as the old
man put it. The way the world measured success, C.E. was
probably right. As sole owner of a rich Nevada mine, C.E.
had not worked to earn a dollar since the early 1860s. Although the silver strike had occurred three years before
Peter Ormond was born, he'd heard about it repeatedly.

His father's wealth was a product of blind luck more than a knowledge of geology or business acumen. C.E. and a partner had borrowed $800 and bought a claim for $1,200. Then the partner had gotten cold feet and backed out, leaving C.E. with a debt of $800 and a trickle of ore, barely capable of providing food. A month later the Comstock Lode was discovered and C.E.'s claim happened to be contiguous to one of the world's richest silver strikes, even sharing some of the same veins. Corny Ormond had at once become C.E. Ormond, prophet and investor, who for the next thirty-nine years had never ceased boasting of his insight and almost psychic powers.

He shivered and started to move toward the stove at the end of the car. But all the seats were taken, so he turned up his collar and thrust his hands into the pockets of his corduroy jacket. Unlike his father, Peter Ormond rarely exercised foresight. Frigid air was lingering later this spring, both in Prescott and St. Louis, and he'd neglected to bring a warm coat. Despite a sickly stomach, his clear head now made him regret the theft of the coins. He mentally replayed the sequence of events that had led up to his spiteful act.

Earlier that evening, silver-haired C.E. Ormond had presided over a table of good food, good company, and animated conversation. The wine went around, and the guests offered numerous toasts, mostly to the good health and long life of their host. Before Peter Ormond realized it, he'd consumed several small glasses of ruby port, mellowing the sharp edges of his sobriety.

After dessert, as the men adjourned to the library, Peter Ormond was feeling reckless. He sat down on the horsehair sofa in front of the fire. Aromatic cigar smoke curled up to mingle with the smell of burning oak and hickory.

". . . damned Spaniards blew up the Maine right there in Havana harbor," a rotund man in evening dress was saying. "Incredible! Killed all those American sailors." He leaned an elbow on the cherry mantel. "It's like they're thumbing their noses at us."

"The Hearst newspapers would have us believe that," a bald man answered mildly. "For all we know it could have been the rag-tag Cuban insurrectionists who are trying to get America to run the Spanish off that island for them. Those Cuban guerrillas knew we would blame the Spaniards for the atrocity."

"Not likely," the first man countered. "I think those arrogant bastards have ruled far too long."

"Which arrogant bastards?" the mild one asked. "The Hearst papers and the War Department?"

"You know who I'm talking about!" the fat man almost yelled. "The Spaniards are kicking up hell in the Philippines, too. We need to put a crimp in their butts . . . run 'em all back to Spain where they belong. They've been spoiling for a fight for a good while. Teddy Roosevelt is right. If America doesn't do it, who will? Our government finally declared war this week . . . two months after the fact!"

"Are you going to enlist?" the bald one asked with a smile.

The rest of the assembly laughed at the ridiculous image this conjured up, while the fat man spluttered a reply and turned to pour himself another drink.

Peter Ormond shifted his attention to a lean guest with silver hair and beard who was talking quietly to C.E. Ormond.

". . . had a bid on a good piece of land in northern California," the man was saying. "But the papers got there a week late. Rotten mail service between here and the West Coast. It's actually worse now than when the Pony Express was running almost forty years ago."

C.E. Ormond smiled thinly. "Maybe Peter the postman could help you with that," he said, squinting through the smoke at his son.

Despite his resolve to stand up to the old man's demeaning jibes, he could think of no rejoinder—nothing cutting or witty enough for a quick reply. Instead, he reached for a glass of pale, dry sherry on the tray carried by Millard Johnson who had ghosted into the library. Ormond lifted his glass in a silent, mock toast to his father. The other men, sensing the tension, gave a few embarrassed chuckles.

He stared out the train window into the darkness. How ironic that the after-dinner sherry should be Amontillado—the very wine that had lured Fortunato to his fate in Edgar Allen Poe's famous story, "The Cask of Amontillado". He knew this wine had given him the reckless courage to perform an act that could very well seal his *own* fate. He'd remained silent in the face of C.E.'s remark, and continued to stare into the fire, knowing he didn't have the quick wit to exchange barbs with his father, especially before an audience. Even if he had, it would have only enraged the old man. C.E.'s sense of humor didn't extend to himself. He had retained a calm exterior, but was boiling inside. Fortunately the blazing logs in the dim room had cast a glow on everyone's countenance, hiding the redness of his face.

He'd had enough. This time the old man would pay. And he had just the plan: hit C.E. where it would embarrass. Steal his pride and joy—his gold coins. They were not just *any* gold coins. They were uncirculated coins struck by various private mints in the West before United States coins were available. The collection consisted of thirty-six pieces—$5, $10, and $20 denominations minted by the

Mormons; Baldwin & Company; Dunbar & Company; the Oregon Exchange Company; Clark, Gruber & Company—all dated between 1849 and 1861. Some were very rare, especially in their perfect condition.

C.E. brought out the coins to show them off at every opportunity. Only a few of his friends at the party had not already seen them. The wives, however, were dazzled. The clink of dessert spoons ceased and the women gasped as the gold coins were arranged on the snowy linen tablecloth. Among the sparkling wine goblets, they gleamed with a rich glow under the light of the big chandelier. They were mounted in thin, custom-made mahogany strips with circular holes cut to accommodate each coin, so the obverse and reverse sides would show. Each polished wooden strip contained six coins, and there were a total of six strips, which could be handled without ever touching the coins themselves.

What would C.E. do when all his friends finally tired of looking at the gold pieces? He'd either have to find some other rarities to flash before awed guests, or find new friends.

Despite locking the safe behind him, he had no hope the missing coins would go undetected for even a day or two. C.E. was a man of regular habits. Every night for as long as he could remember the old man had a glass of milk with soda crackers before bedtime. While enjoying this odd nightcap for the sake of his ulcers, he always opened the safe to gaze one last time on his treasure.

Peter Ormond smiled grimly at the shock and consternation C.E. would experience when he opened the depository concealed behind the oil portrait of himself in the uniform of a Captain of Volunteers. An empty safe behind an empty man. Appropriate.

16

"That'll shake up the old man's digestion," he muttered aloud.

It was well past midnight, so C.E. had likely already sent a servant to roust out the night duty desk sergeant at the nearest police precinct.

While the train swayed and clacked through the darkness, he began to feel better about his action—possibly because his stomach and head were recovering. He never before realized how much a man's outlook on life was affected by his state of health. He tried to analyze how liquor could affect one's judgment. The tangled mesh of cause and effect had somehow culminated in a fateful decision. A maze of circumstances—actions and reactions, something said, minor decisions made—all had to occur in a certain exact pattern to bring him to the brink of stealing those coins. If any one of these preceding events had been slightly altered, he would not have rifled the safe. It was all too complex for his tired brain to unravel. Fate, fortune, chance—whatever it was, had terminated in a deed he would not have done, except for the influence of the wine. But, in the silence of his mind, he could hear the mocking voice of his friend, Arizona ranch foreman, Charley Gunderson: "It ain't the last drink that makes you drunk. It's the six you had before."

"You're right, Charley," he muttered to himself. "Who the hell am I kidding, anyway?" He had to admit that he'd so far been a disappointment to his father. At age thirty-six, he'd done exactly nothing with his life. As the eldest of three, the only son, he felt an obligation to carve out his own niche, however small. After a series of dead-end jobs, he was now a temporary postal clerk in Prescott, Arizona Territory. He hated manual labor of more than a few days' duration. He'd been a single-jack miner once. It'd hardened

17

his muscles, but broken his spirit. He'd swamped in saloons—another dirty job. He'd held horses and shined boots and clerked in a dry goods store. Time killers all, that led nowhere. These jobs had served to keep him fed while he pondered and searched and assessed his own interests and skills. He was a voracious reader, a trait he'd inherited from his lovable and forgiving mother. His formal schooling had extended two years into college. But his love of reading would not earn him a living. If he were ever to find himself, it would be for his mother's sake, not for C.E.'s. He wondered if his father'd had the same personality years ago when he was a poor, young prospector. Or, had sudden wealth brought out his latent arrogance? He couldn't imagine his mother marrying such a man.

"Tickets!"

The conductor's voice jarred him from his reverie. The lean, mustached trainman examined the ticket for an unduly long time before punching it in two places. "To Topeka, then transfer to the Atchison, Topeka, and Santa Fe. . . ." The conductor's deep-set blue eyes bored into him from under the stiff brim of the pillbox cap as he handed back the ticket.

He nodded, trying to appear nonchalant, but cringed inside under the conductor's intense gaze. What had the man seen? He was concerned that there was something suspicious about his appearance. Were the coins making a bulge in his pocket? Had a notice been wired ahead to be on the look-out for a thief of his description? He took a deep breath to calm his nervousness. It was only his guilty conscience. He wasn't accustomed to being a criminal on the run. Such were his imaginings that he half expected the conductor to return with a railroad detective and put him in manacles at gunpoint.

He had not taken the coins for personal gain, he rationalized, and had no intention of keeping or selling them. In a couple of weeks, he'd return them via Wells Fargo express, insured. He just wanted the old man to sweat for a while. A stunt like this would not improve their relationship, but neither would anything else.

He surreptitiously slid two of the strips out of the velvet bag in his pocket and looked at them. Except for some slight variations, most of the coins were similar in design to gold coins from the United States Mint, with the spread eagle on the reverse and the head of Liberty on the front. However, the obverse of the Clark, Gruber & Company $20 coin depicted a pointed mountain with the words **Pikes Peak Gold** around the outside and **Denver** stamped below the mountain.

The coins from Oregon featured a beaver on the obverse. The Mormon coins showed a pair of clasped hands on one side and a beehive on the other. Those symbols indicated productivity and co-operative effort. Brigham Young was the instigator of the early 1849 coinage system and had personally supervised the mint that was housed in a small adobe building in Salt Lake City. In fact, the Mormon $20 gold piece was the first of that denomination to be coined in the United States.

It had been five years since C.E. called in an appraiser to evaluate these rare gold pieces. At that time the market price was set at $51,000. No doubt the numismatic value had increased with the passage of time since these coins would never again be minted, and these particular specimens were not marred or worn by circulation. Gold and land would always have value, since no more of it could be created. C.E. had purchased the coins when they were new. "More beautiful than a printed stock certificate," he was fond of saying. "And more durable, too."

To equalize the weight that was bulging his pocket like a forty-ounce revolver, Ormond removed the coins from the velvet bag, slid two of the strips into his trouser pocket, and the other four into the side pocket of his corduroy jacket.

He became suddenly aware that an attractive, dark-haired woman, seated next to a big man across the aisle, was staring at him. Their eyes met and she quickly looked away. The effects of the wine were wearing off, but his normal caution had not returned. Since these coins had always been in his father's house, he'd come to view them as objects of art, rather than something with great monetary value. He'd have to be more conscious of guarding this valuable treasure. He patted his only personal weapon, a sheath knife on his belt under the jacket. However, he believed that, as long as he took normal precautions, he had no fear of being robbed in a public place.

He glanced about, but everyone was either reading or dozing. He got up to go relieve himself at the convenience near the rear of the car, and nodded as he passed by the young woman. But she evidently didn't notice. She appeared several years junior to her traveling companion. Was he husband, father, or stranger to the woman? The idle thought crossed his mind as he passed them.

Returning to his seat, he touched the lump in his pocket. For all he knew, C.E. had purchased these coins as an investment in the beginning, but now they might be a hedge against a falling silver market. William Jennings Bryan had run for President two years ago on a free silver platform, but had been defeated by William McKinley, a staunch advocate of the gold standard. C.E.'s motives were his own. Only one thing was certain—he had the old man's valuable collection safely in his pockets.

He yawned. The hour was late. He had no watch, but guessed it was close to two in the morning. He wedged himself into the corner by the window and closed his eyes as the train clicked over the rail joints, rolling westward into the night.

"Is this seat taken?"

The musical voice brought him back from the verge of sleep. "Why, no, ma'am. Help yourself." He was pleased to see the young, dark-haired woman he'd noticed earlier.

She murmured her thanks, sliding a small valise beneath the seat, and sank down with a sigh.

"Did you get on at the last stop?" he asked.

"No, I boarded at Saint Charles," she replied in a low voice, brushing her long black hair over one shoulder with a gloved hand. "I was sitting over there, but that half-drunk salesman was trying to molest me."

"Oh?"

"Tried to get me to nip at his flask with him. Wanted to throw a blanket over us so he could paw me. I guess a woman traveling alone is considered fair game."

"Did you complain to the conductor?"

"No sense creating a scene. As long as there are empty seats available, it's easier just to get up and move."

Without being obvious, he studied the young woman in the light of the dimmed overhead lamps. The salesman certainly had good taste. A very attractive package—dark hair and eyes, straight nose. She smelled of scented soap and fresh air. A floor-length blue dress, pinched at the waist, emphasized her slender figure. She carried a long coat and threw it over herself. "Don't let me bother you," she said, wiggling into a comfortable position and closing her eyes.

Tired as he was, Ormond wanted to be bothered by her.

With gray cloth gloves covering her hands, he couldn't tell if she wore a wedding ring. He guessed her age at about thirty. He wondered how far she would be traveling. He made a couple of attempts at conversation, but finally gave it up when she was unresponsive, and it was obvious she wanted to sleep.

Once more he leaned into the corner and closed his eyes. Time enough in the morning to strike up an acquaintance. He would have to start traveling more. Attractive, unattached women were at a premium in Prescott.

"Sir! Wake up!"

Peter Ormond gradually came back from a long way off. The conductor was gently shaking his shoulder. "This is your stop. Topeka."

"Oh. What time is it?" His neck was stiff and his left arm was partially asleep.

"Six-twenty."

He stretched and rubbed his arm. "Where's the woman who was sitting here?"

"She got off in Kansas City."

He felt a pang of disappointment. "Thanks." He stood up, and realized there was no weight in his corduroy coat. His hands slapped at his side pockets. Empty.

"Damn!"

"What is it?" the conductor asked.

"They're gone!" Panic seized him.

"What?"

He searched frantically. Two of the six wooden strips were still in the side pocket of his trousers. The other four were missing from his jacket pocket.

"I've been robbed!" he cried. "What was that woman's name?"

"Beats me," the conductor said. "Thought maybe you knew her."

"No! She picked my pocket of some gold coins. I've got to find her. The railroad's responsible."

"Unless you checked them into the express car safe, the company is not responsible for any personal valuables," the conductor said. "Sorry. You might be able to find out her name if you know where she bought her ticket. But even then, if she's a thief, she could have used an alias. I think you're just out of luck."

"Those coins didn't belong to me. They're worth thousands of dollars!"

Ormond's voice began to rise in panic, and several passengers grumbled something about keeping down the noise.

"Mister, I'm sorry for your loss, but carrying something like that around in your pocket is just asking for trouble."

"I know." He glanced back and noticed the fat salesman was also gone. Coincidence?

"Topeka, Kansas, next stop!" the conductor announced, moving away. "Thirty minute stop here, ma'am," he said to a woman farther along. He departed through the end door.

He slumped back into his seat, pressed down by the weight of overwhelming loss. He thrust his hands into the crevices of the velvet seat, then scanned the floor in a vain hope that perhaps the heavy coins had dropped out of his pocket while he slept. There was little doubt she'd stolen them. What to do? Get off and take the first train back to Kansas City? No good. He didn't know her name and, even though he'd gotten a good look at her, he stood no chance of finding a stranger in a big city. If, by some miracle, she could be located, he had no proof she'd stolen anything. It would be his word against hers.

The train slowed and ground to a halt. With one last

look around, he started toward the door. His only luggage—a small grip—had been left at his parents' house. He and two other passengers climbed down from the car. Four gas lamps glowed in the frosty air at intervals along the depot platform. The gray chill beyond the lights matched his mood. With gritty eyes and sour mouth, he entered the empty waiting room. It smelled of old coal smoke and cigars. The big chalkboard on the wall had been updated to show his train was thirty minutes late. He found himself wishing there were a saloon nearby, but then remembered that Kansas was dry. Probably just as well. Having more to drink would hardly ease the pain. Two-thirds of his father's collection was missing, and no amount of alcohol would kill that memory.

He slumped down on a bench in the vacant waiting room. It was 6:40 a.m. by the big wall clock. Dawn was streaking the overcast sky.

Instead of bearing him southwest across New Mexico to Flagstaff, he fervently wished the Atchison, Topeka, and Santa Fe train would whisk him off to the other side of the world, away from all his troubles.

"Millard, get in here!" C.E. Ormond shouted.

"Yes, sir." The Negro servant entered the spacious library that now seemed suddenly smaller. The dying fire still warmed the comfortable room, insulated by three walls of head-high bookcases and furnished with a couch and six leather armchairs.

"Close the door."

The edge in C.E.'s voice gave Johnson a prickly chill. What had he done? Nothing, that he could think of. He closed the door and stood a respectful ten feet from C.E. Even though he'd been a house servant for the old man for

twenty years, Millard Johnson had never called him anything but "Mister Ormond", or "Sir". Cornelius Edwin Ormond was not one to encourage familiarities from
servants—or family members.

C.E. remained silent for several seconds, his flushed face
working as if in pain. Johnson heard the muffled sound of
the hall clock chiming. It then struck one. Johnson, nearly
fifty-one years old, had put in a long day, attending to many
details for the birthday dinner party that already seemed
like a distant memory. He wished C.E. would dismiss him
to go to bed, but the theft of the prized coins had stuck in
the old man's craw.

Born a slave in 1847, Johnson had never known his father. After the war, his mother had seen some hard times,
going from job to menial job, finally ending as a domestic
for a wealthy family before her death from pneumonia when
Johnson was twenty. Johnson was doing general labor for a
kindly storekeeper, stocking supplies and driving a delivery
wagon. After a year, the owner's wife took an interest in
teaching the young black man to read and write. Johnson
took it from there, eagerly reading whatever he could get his
hands on, and eventually gave himself a spotty education.
But his greatest asset was a disposition that allowed him to
get along with nearly anyone. A slight youngster, he'd gradually built himself up with proper food and hard work. By
the time he'd started working for C.E. he was a lean, muscular thirty-year-old. When Ormond hired him, he'd remarked that Johnson, in his present, marvelous condition,
would have brought at least $1,600 at the New Orleans
slave market before the war.

"Yes, sir," Johnson had replied, inwardly cringing at the
thought. He'd intended to work only long enough to get a
stake to go off prospecting in the Black Hills country. But

he'd fallen in love, married, and wound up staying at his present job for twenty years. After his wife and baby died in childbirth, leaving him again alone in the world, Johnson had accepted C.E.'s offer to let him live in an unused attic room of the Ormond mansion—at reduced wages.

Another gold rush was now under way—this time to the Yukon. But his dreams of wealth and riches from the earth had evaporated with age and inertia. C.E. wasn't the easiest person to work for, and he had never gotten over the idea that all people of color—Indians, Negroes, Chinese—were somehow inferior. But at least the employment here was steady, if demeaning. But being demeaned had never bothered Johnson. He was his own man who kept his own counsel. He knew what and who he was, and didn't let external events or others' attitudes interfere with his inner core of calm self-confidence.

So he awaited C.E.'s orders with only a slight quiver of anticipation and curiosity. It had been years since he'd seen his employer so angry and upset. As he regarded C.E.'s flushed face, Johnson gave thanks that he'd never let gold fever get its hooks into him. And he hoped this business of the coin theft had nothing directly to do with him. Since no culprit had been apprehended, it would be typical of C.E. to blame someone else, and Johnson was handy. He stood impassively, bracing himself for the accusation of negligence. What came next surprised him.

"Millard, after discussing this with the police and thinking it over for a couple of hours, I've come to a conclusion I don't like . . . that no-good son of mine stole my collection."

The old man's jaw was working as he looked down at the floor. Johnson realized how difficult it must be for C.E. to admit to a black servant that his own flesh and blood could not be trusted. He discreetly said nothing and waited.

The old man collected himself and went on. "And on my birthday, too!" The pain on his face was evident.

Johnson wished he were somewhere else.

"I want you to go after him. He's probably on his way back to Prescott in the Arizona Territory. It's a good distance, but you can catch up to him. See if he'll admit to taking the coins. He's known you since he was fifteen, and always liked you. But don't go easy on him. Use the threat of physical force if you have to. Or the law." He paused, his face showing pain, and put a hand to his midsection as if he were about to vomit. "I can't get the law to do anything without some proof . . . other than my word, or my hunch. There was no violence, no damage to the safe. No one took the coins at gunpoint. There were no witnesses. A damned sneak thief took them!" He slammed his fist on the small library desk and his voice rose. "I should never have mentioned Peter as a suspect. Now the police have concluded it's only a family matter. Oh, they'll do a routine follow-up and question all the people who were here tonight . . . but they told me they had no jurisdiction if my son has left the city. The best they can do is send a telegram to the sheriff's office in Yavapai County, Arizona, telling him Peter is wanted for questioning."

Johnson cleared his throat. "Mister Ormond, I'm no detective."

"I know that!" the old man snapped. "You don't have to be. I want you to catch up to him. Use persuasion. Make him see the error of his ways. God knows, I've never been able to. I could hire a private detective, of course, but I'd rather keep this within the family."

And save money, Johnson thought. Wealth had never allowed the old man to let go of pinching nickels—either an old habit, or an inborn stinginess—one of his least attractive traits. Johnson tried to think of some other reason to excuse himself from this onerous duty. He was a servant and didn't relish the idea of getting between this man and his grown son. As he saw it, he had nothing to gain. "Sir, if Peter took the coins, he might not return to Prescott."

"I know, I know. Ask questions at the depot to see if anyone remembers him changing his return ticket."

"Sir, I would do 'most anything for you or Peter. But, if it's all the same to you, I'd rather not get involved in this."

"It's *not* all the same to me! I'm ordering you to go," C.E. growled. He was in no mood to be trifled with by a black servant. "If you refuse, you'll be on the street looking for a job by morning."

"Yes, sir."

"Pack your duffel and I'll drive you to the depot right now. If it'll make you feel any better, I'll make the inquiries at the ticket window. All you have to do is get on the next train to wherever he's headed and fetch me those coins. Is that clear?"

"Yes, sir."

"I'd go myself, but I'm afraid of what I might say or do if I got hold of that miserable ingrate!" His face reddened in the glow of the dying coals on the hearth. He raked his fingers through his long, silver hair, and took a deep breath to steady himself. "That's all. Meet me in the carriage house in ten minutes."

"Yes, sir." Johnson nodded and backed to the door. He'd handled many problems in his life, and could handle this, too, but he was glad his late wife was not here to see it. Ophelia had been a woman of good sense. She would've strongly objected to his going, even though he had no choice.

He closed the library door and trudged up the carpeted stairs to his third floor room, wondering if Mrs. Ormond was aware of the old man's decision. C.E. tended to ignore her as if she were one of the hired hands. A lovely, caring woman, Johnson thought, but not assertive in the least. Probably why their marriage had lasted so long—they seldom butted heads as he and Ophelia had done.

He paused to rest his aching legs before he reached the top of the second flight of stairs. His heart was pounding. Maybe domestic service *was* making him soft. This assignment might just be what he needed to restore some of his physical and mental toughness.

He opened the door to his small room under the slanted eave and sat on the bed to remove his shoes and change into traveling clothes. He smiled to himself. He'd already begun to think of this as an adventure. At least he'd be away from the lash of the old man's tongue for a time—maybe even weeks, depending on where the chase led him. He dragged a ratty suitcase from under the bed and undid the straps. In spite of C.E.'s wanting to avoid a family scandal and to save the expense of hiring an outside detective, Johnson had to admit the old man trusted him. Trusted him enough to intervene in this delicate family matter, using his own judgment and, if successful, to bring back gold coins worth $50,000. But Johnson didn't fool himself into thinking his status had changed. It was the same kind of trust C.E. would put in a faithful, well-trained hunting dog.

Chapter Two

At dusk Peter Ormond stepped off the day coach in Prescott, stiff and tired from the long ride. Thank God, there was a train that connected the territory, north to south, and he didn't have to travel by horseback or rented buggy from the main line in Flagstaff down through rugged Oak Creek Cañon. He'd also saved expenses by not acquiring a Pullman berth.

A spring snow was falling heavily, big, wet flakes melting as they touched the ground. He tugged down on his hat brim and stepped off the depot platform into the street. Since he'd lost most of his father's collection, he looked upon the remaining twelve gold coins as pocket change, hardly worth the effort to guard, even though they were worth upwards of $17,000. He carried no gun for protection and had no ready cash to buy one *en route*. But he did have his eye on a new Bisley model Colt here in Prescott.

It was good to be back in familiar surroundings. He paused for a long minute, savoring the silence and the feathery snowfall in the dead air. Just ahead of him, the solid courthouse dominated the center of town. Although he knew at least two nearby saloons and a hotel were open, the town seemed to have ceased all activity—holding its breath. The streets were deserted. It was the supper hour and most people were home, probably seated around a fire, maybe warming up with hot chili or coffee.

He trudged another block to his adobe house. Making sure no one was lurking in the shadows, he unlocked the plank door and entered the chill, damp dark. Crouching in the back of his mind was the vague fear of being hunted, as if all the bandits in the territory and the police knew he was carrying stolen gold. *How strange the imagination is!* He fumbled to light a coal-oil lamp on the table. The wick flared up, bathing the empty room in warm light, dispelling some of the gloom and dread in his heart. He replaced the smoky chimney and looked around at the silent, empty space he called home. A profound sense of loneliness and loss overcame him. And it wasn't just because of the stolen coins and fear of retribution. Every month, every year that he spent alone, made it more difficult for him to remain self-sufficient and self-sustaining. Maybe it was because he lacked a goal in life—nothing he'd found worthy of his devoted interest and energy. Were humans social creatures by nature? He'd always considered himself something of a loner. Perhaps selfishness was the reason. He met a lot of people at the post office where he was presently employed, but no eligible women near his age.

He resolved to get out more—buy a horse, work on his riding skills, take some trips into the surrounding desert, read up on gemstones, learn more about wildlife, or *something*. Prospecting held no interest, since any thought of mining brought unpleasant memories of his father.

He brushed away the mental cobwebs shadowing his mood. They came mostly when he was weakened by fatigue and hunger. He quickly set about building a fire in the cook stove and slicing some bacon. The small sticks of juniper and mesquite gradually caught and blazed up. He removed two of the stove lids so the fragrant fire could begin to warm the room. There was plenty of wood in the woodbox, and, after supper, he'd kindle a fire in the corner beehive fireplace.

As he ate beans and bacon with a few stale crackers, he brightened up, and again faced the dilemma of where to hide the remaining coins. If taking the collection was intended to shake up the old man, it was actually working in reverse. Now he had been the victim of a sneak thief. But that fact would not deter the police from dogging his trail. He'd better have some plausible story ready in case the sheriff confronted him. Perhaps he'd just tell the truth and say he was planning to return the collection, but that two-thirds of it had been stolen. A completely implausible tale, even though true. Maybe he'd wrap the two remaining strips for shipment right away by Wells Fargo. No. Better to let C.E. sweat a little first. When he did send them, he'd include a note telling the old man exactly what happened. C.E. thought so little of his son's capabilities, the old man would probably believe the story.

In the meantime, he had to come up with a good place to conceal them. He finished his meal, and shoved the dishes aside on the table. He turned up the wick of the lamp to examine the remaining twelve coins. He'd seen them many times before, but the crisp, finely struck designs in gold never failed to fascinate him. They were not an obsession, as they were with his father, but, nevertheless, he enjoyed looking at anything of beauty.

"Nobody who has an eye for beauty will ever be bored with life," he'd heard his father say. It was one of the few things the old man probably had right. He sat staring numbly at the twelve remaining coins mounted in the two mahogany strips. He was tired. Where should he stash them for the night? The golden works of art were already becoming a burden to him. Finally he decided to wrap them in a cotton towel and bury them in the bottom of the woodbox. Probably the first place anyone would look in this one-room house, but they were out of sight until morning. He'd find a better place then. Using a shovel full of coals from the cook stove, he kindled a fire in the beehive fireplace in the corner of the room. Then he settled into a padded wicker rocker—his one concession to luxury—to read by the light of the lamp. He found his place in a borrowed copy of Mark Twain's *Following the Equator*. For a half hour he was transported beyond the adobe walls and traveled by train with Twain as he lectured across India. His eyelids finally growing heavy, he set the book down, undressed, turned out the lamp, and sought the solace of the blankets on his bunk.

He awoke at daylight, well rested after eight hours of sleep. Beyond his window was a white world covered with two inches of snow. Although the sun had yet to break from the horizon, the sky was clear. Warmed-over coffee and bacon were his breakfast. He was about out of foodstuffs. Pay day was tomorrow, time to replenish his supplies.

Then he remembered the gold coins, and his mood plummeted. What would he tell his father? Even if C.E. didn't have him prosecuted and sent to jail, Ormond felt morally obligated to make restitution. Repaying the loss in dollars would likely take him the rest of his life. He retrieved the coins from the woodbox. After some searching, he discovered a narrow crack at the base of the adobe wall where the house had settled, creating a slender opening at the floorboards. He found a stack of old newspapers he used to start fires in the cook stove. The two-month-old paper on top screamed in bold print for vengeance against the Spanish for blowing up the *Maine* and assorted atrocities. Old news. Ormond hadn't seen a newspaper since leaving St. Louis, but had heard talk on the train that volunteers from the Arizona Territory were gathering at old Whipple Army Barracks here on the outskirts of Prescott. Gossip had it that these men would join other volunteers from the Territorial West to make up a cavalry regiment to fight in Cuba. War talk was in the air. But he felt detached from it. Whatever happened, it didn't affect him, he thought; he had troubles of his own.

He folded several sheets of newspaper around the strips of coins and slid them into the crack. Then he stood and looked at the spot. Perfect. If anyone saw the tiny edge of newspaper protruding, they'd take it for stuffing to keep out the cold air.

He finished, put on his long duster and hat, and, judging the time of day from the sun's appearance on the horizon, left for work, locking the door behind him. He shuffled through two inches of new snow toward the post office, breathing the fresh air and wishing he didn't have to spend the day indoors. But most jobs he could do, that weren't physical labor, were inside. He could be a work slave anywhere. It didn't have to be in a beautiful setting like this. He had selected Prescott, not only because of its scenic surroundings, but because of its elevation. It was about halfway between Phoenix and Flagstaff, high enough to escape the blistering heat of the desert floor, yet not at an elevation that brought on suffering from extreme cold and snow in winter. To him, Prescott seemed ideal in the matter of weather. And his moods were greatly affected by the weather. Even though he would rather have spent his days doing something besides sorting mail and various other odd jobs, he consoled himself that this temporary position would end in six weeks. Then what? Typically he had put off thinking that far ahead. Probably just drift on to something else, as he always did. Maybe, since three-quarters of his father's coins had already been stolen from him, he should just sell the rest and live on the $10,000 to $15,000 they'd probably bring. His basic honesty rejected this idea almost immediately. Even if he were so inclined, coins of this rarity and value would be relatively easy to trace, unless he found some wealthy collector who would keep his mouth shut.

By lunchtime he was nearly back into the rhythm of work. To a person of his temperament, with a lazy streak, any kind of work was like exercise—the longer one was away from it, the harder it was to start back again.

"Peter, aren't you going to break for lunch?" Rodney Harrison, his balding supervisor stuck his head in the door.

"Just going." He flipped the last two letters into pigeonholes and reached for his duster. He'd have to buy a cheap watch if he were going to continue working at jobs regulated by the clock instead of by the task, he thought as he crossed the street to take advantage of the free lunch at a nearby saloon.

He bought a beer, then made himself a ham and cheese sandwich from the food at the end of the bar. To escape the noise and cigar smoke, he took his food and mug and stepped outside into the sunshine. Squinting at the sun's blinding reflection off the snow, he noticed bare patches of earth here and there. The street was churned to slushy mud by the passing horses and wagons. Snow melt ran off roofs in driblets and streams as the sun beat back this latest onrush of winter. The trees in St. Louis would be budding in the April sunshine. But St. Louis was one place he didn't want to think about just now. He munched his sandwich and sipped the beer, relishing the warmth of the sun's reflection off the snow.

He finished eating, returned the mug, then walked a half block to Wilson's Gun Shop. And this time he wasn't window-shopping. He owned an early 1873 model Colt .45 Army revolver that had been given to him when his friend, ranch foreman Charley Gunderson, bought himself a new one. The gun had been good in its day, a quarter century ago. But it had seen much hard use and was not as tight as it had been. Some of the bluing had worn off, and its wood grips were scuffed. The weapon was still usable, but Rufus Wilson, the gun dealer, had his eye on it for potential antique value, due to its very low serial number.

"You still got that Bisley Colt I was looking at, Rufus?" Ormond asked, closing the shop door behind him.

"Sure do." The young gunsmith smiled, setting down the shotgun he was working on and stepping out front to the counter. "Haven't seen you for a couple of weeks. Thought maybe you lost interest in it."

"Nope. Just went home for a visit." He bent down to look at the new, ivory-gripped, nickel-plated Colt in the display case. The price tag hanging from the trigger guard showed a figure well beyond his reach.

"Want to take a look at it?" Wilson inquired.

"Nope. I've drooled over it enough. Would you consider a trade . . . say, my old Army Colt, plus twenty dollars for the Bisley?"

"You got the gun with you?"

"Yeah." He pulled the Colt from the pocket of his duster and handed it over.

Wilson examined it closely, working the action. Then he

pulled the pin and slipped out the cylinder, held the piece to the light and looked down the barrel.

"You've got a deal," he said, reassembling the weapon.

Ormond broke into a grin. "Thanks."

Wilson handed over the Bisley and Ormond paid him. They shook hands on it.

"How about a holster and ammunition?" Ormond asked, admiring the graceful scrollwork engraved on the cylinder and part of the barrel.

"I think I've got an old holster back here that will fit it until you can find something better. One box of shells enough?"

"Yes."

"Let's see . . . that's a Thirty-Two-Twenty," Wilson said, looking along a shelf stacked with boxes. "A very popular caliber. Not sure why. Leastways, Colt seems to be making a lot of the Bisleys in that size so far."

The deal sealed, Ormond thanked Wilson and left the shop with the bright new Bisley strapped to his belt.

As he crossed the street, stepping around the worst mud holes, worries about his future again intruded on his thoughts. He thought of Rufus Wilson. The well-liked gun dealer, seven to eight years his junior, was married and had two children. The man leased the building where he owned his own business and seemed to be making a good living. His was a skill in demand in the West, even though the raw frontier had given way to ranching and the towns nurtured most other occupations found in Eastern cities. The clock was ticking for Ormond. At age thirty-six, he was past due for settling into some career.

Ormond sighed and brought his attention back to the present. He would enjoy his new prize. Pausing by the back door of the post office, he slid his Bisley out of its holster.

Many men did not like the look or feel of the new grip and the flatter hammer that Colt had introduced only two years before, after prototypes scored extremely well at the shooting matches in Bisley, England. But the new design fit Ormond's hand perfectly. Knowing that he would eventually buy it, Wilson had let him take it out into the desert and shoot it. A natural marksman, Ormond was extremely accurate with the weapon, even given its shorter 4¾-inch barrel—the same length as the ejector.

As he reholstered the gun and opened the back door of the post office, he realized that this new gun was not just a toy. Even though many men still went armed, he'd never felt the need for personal protection here in Prescott—until now, when he had to protect stolen gold. Tomorrow was pay day and he would recoup his meager finances depleted by the trip to St. Louis.

"The mail stage just arrived," Rodney Harrison told him as he came in. "A full sack for us to sort."

Ormond nodded.

"What's the matter? You look a little peaked. Something you had for lunch not agree with you?" Harrison asked, looking up from under his green eyeshade.

"Yeah." His lunch sat on his stomach like a lump of coal. "Strange. I can usually eat anything and it never bothers me. Maybe it was that pickled egg I had at the saloon."

"Those eggs been in that jar on the bar since before I came to town. Rumor has it they're dinosaur eggs." Harrison chuckled. "Well, buck up, 'cause there's a fella out here to see you."

"What?" Ormond's stomach gave a sudden twinge. "Who?"

"Don't know. Leathery looking. Said he just got into

38

town, and it was urgent he see you." He jerked a thumb toward the front of the building. "He's a waitin' out there."

"Rod, I've got to go use the outhouse before I see anybody," Ormond said, putting a hand to his midsection. "He'll have to wait a few more minutes."

He stepped out the back door and across the alley to the privy. Safely inside, he dropped his pants and sat down. Then he carefully loaded the Colt Bisley and tested the action. Good. Wilson had cleaned and oiled this gun since Ormond had practiced with it. He had no intention of shooting anyone; it was only for protection in the most extreme emergency. Before showing himself, he resolved to get a look at this visitor. He wasn't expecting anyone. If a lawman or Pinkerton detective was already on his trail, it was very fast police work. Ormond knew he should never have returned to Prescott; it was the first place they would come looking for him. He had no intention of being charged, jailed, indicted, and tried for something that had started out as a prank. "Damn!" he breathed. If only he still had all the coins to return!

He tore a page from the ratty Sears, Roebuck catalogue hanging from a cord to conclude his business, then got up and adjusted his clothing, swinging the long duster over the holstered gun.

Stepping outside, he cautiously circled the post office building to see the man who was asking for him. If necessary, he could always flee, abandon his job and get out of town. He had two weeks' pay coming, but that could be collected later. First things first.

He inhaled deeply and turned the corner to peer inside through the glass of the front window.

Chapter Three

A tall man in a long duster and wide-brimmed hat stood with his back to the front window, reading a Wanted poster on the wall. For a long minute Ormond fidgeted, his stomach knotting, as he waited for the figure to move and reveal his face. Judging from the streaked linen duster and sweat-stained hat, this could very well be some hard-riding lawman sent to track him down.

The man finally turned to take a seat in the captain's chair by the front door, and Ormond's breath rushed out in relief. It was his friend, Charley Gunderson, foreman of the Double X Ranch just north of Tucson.

Ormond flung open the door. "Charley, what brings you up this way? By God, it's good to see you!" Ormond rushed on, pumping the foreman's callused hand. Gunderson, having stood up, pushed back his hat. Wind and sun had tanned his lean face, and the thick, blond hair needed a trim, a three-day growth of stubble bristled on his chin, but he was the picture of outdoor health.

"I just rode in," the foreman said, glancing around at two other customers in line to mail packages at a caged window. "Is there some place we can talk? I've got something to tell you."

"Outside." Ormond led the way into the chilly sunshine, and the two men stepped around to the side of the building that bordered an empty street.

"I've got a proposition for you," the taller man said with no preliminaries.

Ormond waited as the foreman paused. A stream of melted snow gurgled along the street.

"You don't have to take it if you're not inclined. But I know you're usually looking to pick up another job or some extra money."

"Yeah."

"I want you to help me and two of the boys drive a herd of wild horses north to the railroad."

"What? I'm no cowboy. Besides, I have a job here."

"You stand to profit by at least two thousand dollars for less than a week's work. I daresay that's more than you'll earn here in a year. But there will be some risk involved."

"Tell me about it."

"I'll have to start at the beginning. You got a few minutes?"

Ormond nodded.

Gunderson paused, his blue eyes staring into the middle distance as he arranged his thoughts. "There's generally not a lot of work on the Double X this time of year . . . mostly just maintenance stuff," he said. "The seasonal hands drifted on and we were skeleton-thin. Even so, I got wind of a rumor that the boss was going to let me go."

"Really? How long you been there?"

Gunderson waved a gloved hand impatiently. "That's not the point. Longevity and a good record have nothing to do with it. The owner did say he was sorry to lose me, but the Army was cutting 'way back on the number of remounts they're planning to buy from us this year." He took a deep breath. "Anyway, me and some of the older wranglers figured we had to do something to insure a little income to tide us over." He smiled grimly. "To quote the opportunistic steward in the Bible parable . . . 'to dig, I was not able; to beg, I was ashamed.' "

If Gunderson was building up to ask for a loan, he was out of luck. The only thing Ormond had of any value were the twelve stolen coins.

"Anyway, to make it short, we drew our time, and the four of us rode off south, toward the Las Guijas Mountains near the border. Five years ago, I discovered a bunch of rare Spanish horses running wild, somehow surviving in that rugged land. Didn't have any help then, so I couldn't catch any of them. But this time, we rounded up a herd of more than a hundred."

"You've got them with you?"

"Corralled in a valley just northeast of here. Been on the trail for more'n two weeks. Meeting a buyer at Ash Fork on the railroad fifty miles north of here."

"So, you've become a mustanger."

"No, you don't understand. This is a one-time thing and these aren't just *any* horses. They're pure-blood Spanish stock that've survived unchanged for three hundred years."

"Hard to believe an undiluted strain could still exist in the wild. Wouldn't they interbreed with escaped cow ponies or cavalry mounts?"

Gunderson nodded. "That's what most people would think. I believe this herd has survived many generations intact because they were so isolated. As I said, I first ran across them by accident five years ago. A couple saddle tramps I met in a saloon told me they'd worked a few of these horses on a ranch the year before. From what they said, I guessed these horses were the real Spanish stock. Later, when I got to town, I scoured the libraries in Tucson and Phoenix. Even read up old ranch records every chance I got. Seems that, back in the Eighteen Sixties a man named Ruben Wilbur . . . a doctor from Harvard, he was . . . worked as a physician for the Cerro Colorado Mining Company. When that outfit went bust, he homesteaded one hundred and forty acres near Arivaca. About ten years later a Mex horse trader, name of Zepulveda, came riding north with six hundred head of Spanish horses, selling them off as he went. Wilbur bought a bunch and turned 'em loose in those rugged cañons on his place, and would just catch one now and again for ranch work."

"What makes these horses so special?" Ormond asked, trying to speed up the story, and wondering when his boss would start yelling for him.

"They're small, but tough. Survive anywhere. Same kind of horses that carried the missionary, Father Kino, hundreds of miles in the late Sixteen Hundreds. Cowhands nicknamed them 'rock horses' 'cause their hoofs are like rocks. Nails would bend when the farriers tried to shoe them. The horses can scale rugged mountain slopes. Yet, they're beautiful and graceful . . . bays, piebalds, blacks . . . all colorations. Blue eyes is even a common trait among 'em."

"They're valuable?"

"Somebody thinks so. The pure strain supposedly became extinct a few years ago. I guess that's why this wealthy buyer wants to take 'em off our hands and ship 'em back East."

"Sounds like you hit the jackpot. You ought to be happy, but you look a little agitated."

"There's only one problem. When I first encountered those horses, I thought they were on open range. Turns out they were still on the spread owned by the descendents of Ruben Wilbur."

"Did the ranch owner know about the horses?"

"Didn't ask, but I suspect so."

"But you and the boys took them, so technically you're rustlers," Ormond summed up.

"That's about it. They're unbranded, but we did have to tear down a brush and pole barricade built across the mouth of an eight-mile-long box cañon."

"So why are you here, and how do I fit into all this?"

"We were bringing the horses up this way, and I thought you might want to throw in with us. Mountain lions got a few along the way, but we still got a herd of more'n a hundred. Figured you could use the money, and frankly we could use an extra hand to get 'em on to Ash Fork. You'd share in the profits."

Ormond was touched. "Thanks for thinking of me, Charley, but I'm not worth a damn in the saddle. Maybe I could be a silent partner." He thought of using the coins as some kind of investment collateral. "Besides, I'm coming in on the tail end of this thing. What would your partners think?"

"I've already cleared it with them," Gunderson said. "Of course, you'd also share in the risk. If we're caught with those animals and accused of rustling . . . well, you know the penalty for that in the territory. Some o' these gun-totin' ranchers catch you with stock they claim as their own, a trial is usually not the first thing on their minds."

Ormond was silent as he thought over the proposition. What did he have to lose? He was already a man on the run. It was also clear to him why Gunderson was making this offer. Friendship had little to do with it. Ormond was an expert shot with a six-gun, and Gunderson knew it. The former ranch foreman probably needed an extra gun for protection. "Where'd you say you're taking them?"

"The buyer's waiting in Ash Fork. Got the stock cars lined out on a siding to ship them East."

"Are the four of you armed?"

Gunderson swung back his duster to reveal a holstered Colt. "Winchesters in saddle scabbards, too."

"Can you give me a couple hours? I've got to resign and see if I can draw my pay a little early, then tell my landlord I'm going."

"Sure. We'll hold the herd where they are overnight. We've been pushing pretty hard, and the animals are tired. Don't want them to be too bony when we get to the railhead."

Ormond reached into his pocket. "Here, take this key. My little rented adobe is just down the street. I'll tell you how to get there. Go let yourself in and stay out of sight until I get off work. Two, three hours. We have to talk. I've got a story to tell you, too."

"Damn!" Gunderson stared at the two strips of gold coins he held. "I . . . you never struck me as the type for this sort of thing." He glanced up sharply at Ormond. The late afternoon sun lanced through the window, lighting up his bronzed face.

"It's amazing what a man will do under duress," Ormond replied, stirring up the fire in the cook stove. He had related the whole story to Gunderson.

"And twenty-four more of these were stolen from you on the train . . . by a *woman?*" He was plainly incredulous.

"Careless and half drunk." Embarrassed, Ormond kept

his back to his friend as he added some wood splinters to the stove. "I went to sleep."

"What now?"

"Don't know. That's why I'm grabbing your offer. I just wanted you to know in case some lawman comes looking for me."

"Yeah. Well, to be right honest with you, we've caught sight of someone dogging our trail, too. If it was a legal posse, out to arrest us for horse stealin', we figure they'd have done it by now. We figure it's probably rustlers out to make a quick buck by taking the horses from us."

"I picked up some bacon, beans, and flour at the store," Ormond said, ignoring this revelation. Regardless of the danger, he was determined to join Gunderson. "Sure you won't stay and eat with me?"

"Thanks, but I've got to get back to the herd. The boys are expecting me. Besides, if those riders we spotted decide to come down on us tonight, even four guns may not be enough. And we got to sleep sometime. It's been a long haul. We swap off night guard. Thanks for the coffee." He tossed the grounds into the fireplace and set his tin cup on the table. "See you out there about dawn, then?"

"You bet. I can't wait to get out of this town."

Gunderson paused at the door, shrugging into his duster. "What're you gonna do with those coins?"

"Bring 'em with me. They don't take up any space."

"Kinda risky, ain't it?"

"Safer than any place I know. The risk was in getting into the old man's safe in the first place. The only other solution would be to rent a safety deposit box at the bank. But, then, I might never get back here."

"Send your father the key and a note," Gunderson suggested.

"He'd have 'em outta there in a week. Then he'd know that two-thirds of them are missing."

"Whatever you think best. See you early." He opened the door. "Be sure you've got that gun I gave you. You could need it."

Ormond pulled the nickel-plated Bisley from his holster that he had traded for it.

Gunderson was impressed. "Good. Me and the boys are each trailing a spare mount, so you can have mine for now. He's probably the gentlest broke, but still a good stock horse."

"Thanks. You can take the rent outta my share of the profits."

"No need. I'll pick up a used saddle at the livery or the mercantile down the street and have it waiting for you." Gunderson waved and shut the door behind him.

Ormond had drawn a check for his separation pay, then signed a paper that stated he was voluntarily terminating his temporary job a few weeks early for personal reasons. The bank was already closed, so he'd have to wait until he reached Ash Fork to cash the check. No matter. He had a few dollars in his pocket—enough to see him through, since there'd be no place to spend any money between here and there, anyway.

He had a sudden premonition of danger and decided to leave tonight instead of in the morning. Maybe he was acquiring outlaw instincts, but he had a strong urge to be gone from this town. He cooked his supper, burning the bacon in his haste to eat and get away. He rolled up a Navajo blanket from the bed and stuffed it, along with a change of clothes, into a canvas duffel. Then he added a razor, a toothbrush, a bar of soap, and the box of cartridges. The coins, in their velvet bag, he slid into his pants pocket.

The new pistol had not been removed from his belt since he'd traded for it at noon. *He travels best who travels light,* he thought, glancing at what he was leaving behind. The utensils and the remaining food someone else could have—maybe a little compensation to the landlord for vacating with only a few hours' notice. He still clung to the amenities of normal life, as if he were not a man on the run—technically an outlaw, in spite of his good intentions to return the coins, most of which he no longer had. Good intentions had no place before the law.

Shouldering the duffel, he went out, leaving the key in the padlock on the door. A weight seemed to slide from his shoulders—the burden of unnecessary possessions, of obligation and responsibility. His remaining life would follow the path of rootlessness if he continued to feel this way, but he didn't care. He was thankful that Gunderson had come along with his offer when he did.

Ormond swung off down the street, eyes and ears alert, like a coyote invading human space. Loping across the town square, he angled north and east, avoiding the few pedestrians. At the edge of town he stepped over the railroad tracks just south of the depot. The afternoon train from Ash Fork was panting quietly at the platform, thirty yards away, unloading passengers and freight. It was the same train from which he'd debarked only twenty-four hours earlier. He paused for a moment and ran his eyes over the squat, 2-6-0 Mogul locomotive painted a royal blue. A beautiful machine. It could carry him south to Phoenix, where he could lose himself in the growing city. Maybe he should just buy a ticket and jump aboard, forgetting all about this horse-herding business with its potential dangers. But he needed the $2,000 Gunderson had promised. And the ranch foreman was a man of his word. Besides, it was already hot in Phoenix and would be sizzling like Hades in another month or two. He turned toward the valley of the wild horses.

"Peter!"

He jumped, a chill running over him at the sound of his own name so close. He looked up, but could see only a dark silhouette against the westering sun.

"No need for that!" the familiar voice said.

Ormond realized his hand was on the butt of his Bisley. He moved to one side to get a better look at the bulky figure that was now blocking the sun's rays. The big man stepped down off the depot platform and moved toward him, removing his hat as he did. "Good to see you," the bass voice rumbled.

Ormond blinked a few times and his vision cleared. There stood Millard Johnson, his father's black servant, a big hand thrust out toward him.

Chapter Four

Ormond was stunned. He looked around quickly for his father.

"I'm alone," the black man said, observing Ormond's apprehensive glance. "C.E. sent me to find you."

"What for?" The question sounded ridiculous, even to his own ears.

"Let's find a place we can talk."

"No time. I'm leaving."

"Even if you're catching this train, you got at least ten minutes," Johnson said, coming toward him.

Ormond shook his head. "Somebody's waiting for me." He was beginning to feel trapped. He had to get away from this man. "Can't talk now. Gotta go." He edged away, and suppressed an urge to take off running. The canvas duffel on his shoulder felt awkward. He didn't want to hurt Johnson's feelings, but he wasn't going back to face C.E. Maybe if he just kept a pokerface and denied everything, Johnson would give up and not call in the sheriff. *Don't act guilty,* Ormond thought. What blind, dumb luck to be hurrying past the depot just as Millard Johnson was getting off the train!

"OK, make it fast. I'm in a hurry." He saw no need to be courteous to this man. Both of them knew why he had come. Ormond needed to bluff his way through. "Over here," he said, leading the way behind the wooden depot into the shade, away from the bustling activity of the passengers and porters on the platform. He eased the bag off his shoulder and set it by his feet.

"It's good to see you, Peter . . . ," Johnson began.

"We just saw each other last week," Ormond cut him off coldly. "What do you want?"

The colored man dropped all pretense at civility. "C.E. want his gold coins back."

"What? His gold coins?" Ormond did a poor job of feigning surprise. "Is the old man getting senile?" he sneered. "Can't keep up with his stuff?"

"He know you took 'em," Johnson said simply, looking directly into Peter Ormond's eyes.

"He knows no such thing. Where's the proof?" He hedged, not making a flat denial. He knew there was no direct evidence against him. The remaining twelve coins were in his trouser pocket at the moment, but this man had no right to search him. Ormond had to convince Johnson he was not the thief, or at least placate or frustrate the man with constant denials so he'd leave and go home without calling in the law. Ormond wished Gunderson would come to his rescue, but the foreman wasn't expecting him until dawn tomorrow.

"You run off that night without sayin' good bye, and the coins come up missin' at the same time. That's all the proof C.E. needs," Johnson said, still fixing Ormond with that disconcerting stare. "If you just hand 'em over, I'll be takin' 'em back without no mo' trouble," he said mildly. "C.E., he be willin' to forgive and forget."

"If he does, it'll be the first time," Ormond scoffed. "I don't have them," he said. Only a partial lie; he didn't have two-thirds of them. "And I don't know where they are." This was certainly the truth, or he'd have gone after them. "Go back and tell C.E. he's hunting the wrong coyote."

The black man heaved a tired sigh and turned to stare off into the distance. "I been knowin' you since you was just a sprout of fifteen. Don't recollect you was ever partial to lying. Fact is, you always told the truth, even when you knew it'd get you into trouble. If you did sumpin' bad, you fessed up and took your lickings like a man." He dragged his gaze back, his somber brown eyes containing a touch of sadness. "Now, you gone and turned into a sneak thief, and a liar to boot."

If he'd been truly innocent, Ormond would have shown some outrage at this accusation, and they both knew it. They stood staring at each other without speaking.

"I don't know what become of you since you growed up. They was a time I was proud of you." He shook his head. "No more," he concluded with a tone of resignation.

Ormond felt a flush of anger at the condescending tone of this black servant. If Johnson had had an ounce of gumption or pride himself, he would have left C.E.'s employ long ago. Groveling servitude was abhorrent to Ormond, who had bucked authority all his life. He couldn't imagine why this man would voluntarily become a wage slave to a tyrant like C.E. Ormond. Possibly it had something to do with Johnson's early years as a slave. Damn C.E. and his coins! And damn this man who'd been sent to take them back.

"So, the old man lost something he prized more than his family!" Revenge was satisfying! "Now he knows how it feels to be hurt. Go back and tell C.E. that I don't have his damned gold trinkets." He shouldered his duffel and turned away. "And tell him I said he's a cheapskate for sending you instead of hiring a Pinkerton man. Typical of the old skinflint!"

"You could have a mite of pity on him," Johnson said. " 'Cause he did give you life."

"And then proceeded to make it a hell! Thanks to him, I've been running from everything since I left home years ago."

"A man on the move all the time generally ain't easy in his mind," Johnson observed.

"That's me, all right."

"C.E.'s gettin' on in years," Johnson continued his original train of thought. "His ulcer been actin' up lately, and this loss makin' it even worse."

"Oh, really?" Ormond sneered. "We can only pray it's serious."

"Every dog has his day, and every man his failin's," Johnson said.

"Meaning what?"

"C.E. be on top for a while, and now he goin' down. Now it be your turn on top. It's what a man does in his prime that matters later. If you keep on this way, you'll regret it someday."

"Ha! You're starting to sound just like him. You been there too long." He turned to leave.

"He didn't call in the law 'cause he wanted to give you a chance to return the coins on your own."

Ormond kept walking.

"Reckon I don't have no choice but to get the sheriff, then," Johnson said, replacing his hat.

Ormond stopped, suddenly, regretting his arrogance. But he couldn't help gloating, as if the old man were here in person. The sheriff or a deputy would go to his house and make a search. They'd likely discover from his landlord where he'd gone. And the herd wasn't due to move until morning. He'd have to hide the twelve coins. This is just what he feared would happen—the law snooping around, possibly arresting him on suspicion of grand theft at Johnson's insistence.

Ormond didn't even know these wranglers with Gunderson. The sheriff might begin to question where the unbranded herd of horses had come from. Ormond didn't want to bring any trouble to Gunderson and his men. He could take off on his own and probably elude pursuit. But then he'd forego the $2,000 Gunderson had promised to pay him. And at the moment he needed that money.

"Millard! Wait!"

The Negro paused.

"If I give you the full story, will you promise to leave the law out of this?"

"You got my word. I can't speak for C.E., but that's why he sent me."

"OK, then, here's what happened. I took the coins from the wall safe. I knew where C.E. had written the combination, so it was no trouble. I'd had a little too much to drink, and the old man's insults got to be more than I could stand. I'd been gone, and forgot what an overbearing bastard he was. Anyway, to get back at him, I grabbed the coins and took off."

"Figured it be somethin' like that." Johnson nodded. "Guess you weren't upstairs in bed like everybody thought."

"I haven't told you the worst of it." Ormond proceeded to detail the theft of the coins on the train by the attractive woman. "I hate to admit to such a stupid blunder, but she got away with twenty-four of the thirty-six coins. I was

54

gonna send the whole bunch of 'em back in a couple weeks, but now I'm not sure what I'll do." He pulled the two strips from his pants pocket. "Here. Take what I have left. Tell him what happened. Knowing him, he'll want a pound of flesh from me for this. But I can tell you, I'll make myself mighty scarce if he sicks the law on me."

Johnson looked thoughtful as he took the coins.

"What's wrong?" Ormond asked after several seconds.

"Tryin' to guess what yo' Daddy gonna say when I tell him this."

"I don't give a damn what he says!" Ormond exploded. "I'm tired of tiptoeing around his moods and his temper and his arrogance."

"Just thinkin' what he'll do to *me*," Johnson said.

" 'Probably shoot the messenger who carries the bad news." Ormond shrugged. "That'd be just like him.'"

"He'll fire me, sure," Johnson went on. "Figure he'll charge me with stealin', like I squirreled away the rest of the coins and just made up that story."

"Well, I'm sorry I took the damned things. I'm sorry some of them were stolen. I'm sorry about the kind of man he is. I'm sorry for a lot of things, but, hell, if this is all about money, he can just collect the insurance, can't he?"

Johnson shook his head, brown eyes wide in his solemn face. "He don't have no insurance on them."

"What? Why? That's crazy!"

"Oh, he had a little at first, years ago. But, time moved on and he didn't see no advantage to it, since the coins never left his house. But the main thing was, the premiums kept goin' up and he didn't want to throw away good money on somethin' he couldn't seem to get no use out of."

Ormond couldn't help grinning at the irony of it. "Done

in by his own greed," he said. "He'd skin a louse for its hide and tallow."

Johnson glanced at the coins in his hand, then slid them into the inside pocket of his gray suit coat.

" 'Booooarrrd!" The conductor's voice came to them from the other side of the depot. *Whoof! Whoof!* Clouds of black smoke billowed above the roof as the locomotive jerked the train into motion.

Johnson took a toothpick from his pocket and stuck it between his lips, as he half turned to stare in the direction of the departing train.

For a time neither man spoke. Ormond felt he had somehow shifted the burden of this whole mess to the shoulders of the older man. It was almost as if he was no longer responsible.

"Look, I'm leaving town. You're welcome to stay at my place tonight before you start back tomorrow." He was beginning to feel sorry for the old servant.

"Much obliged, but I won't be goin' back tomorrow."

"Why's that?"

"The way I see it, if you be tellin' me the honest-to-God truth, I'm in a pretty tight place."

"Hell, just tell him you couldn't find me. Let me have those coins back and I'll mail them to him with a letter from some little, one-horse town far from here."

"Can't rightly do that . . . I don't hold with lyin'."

"Even if it would save your job? He knows you're not a professional lawman. He'd believe it if you said you never found me."

The older man sadly shook his head as if it were out of the question. "This done happened for a reason. The Lord Almighty knows that reason, but I got to figure me a way out o' this."

The sun had disappeared and the shadows were blending into dusk.

"Where you goin' now?" Johnson asked.

Ormond debated whether or not to tell him. "You've struck a rock on this truth business, haven't you? Well, if you must know, I'm joining with a friend who's got a few horses corralled out here in the valley. I've hired on to help drive the herd north to the railroad."

"There's a railroad right here."

"The buyer's waiting in Ash Fork, about fifty miles north at the junction where you just changed trains."

"Reckon they'd mind if an old black man rode along? Maybe I could sort things out in the fresh air and decide what to do by the time we get there."

"I don't know. . . ." Ormond was dubious.

"I could rent a saddle horse from the livery. And I'm a good cook."

"Let me go out there and ask. Get you a good seat in the depot waiting room. If I'm not back by midnight, you can figure the answer is no, and I'm not coming back."

"Fine by me."

By the time two wranglers rode in from night herd to awaken their replacements just after midnight, Millard Johnson had become a member of the crew. He was adding a handful of grounds and a little water to freshen up the coffee in the blackened pot steaming over glowing coals. Besides Gunderson, the three others were called simply Red, Sparky, and José.

Red, a tall, freckled man in his late thirties, wore a permanent scowl. Sparky, shorter and stockier with a round face, had a more congenial attitude. José was handsome, about twenty-five, with a drooping mustache; he seemed to take more pride in his appearance than the others, even though they all wore leather chaps and vests. José sported a white shirt, along with a thin silver turquoise bracelet. He was a keen observer, but kept to himself most of the time.

Ormond squatted by the fire and studied Johnson, but could read nothing in the poker expression of the face that shone like polished mahogany in the firelight.

"No night herding for you until you get used to the saddle," Gunderson said, mounting up to take his turn on watch. Ormond nodded, glad of the chance to get some sleep. He could hardly hold his eyes open.

"Boys, this here is Millard Johnson," Gunderson said from horseback to Red and Sparky. "He'll be with us to Ash Fork as cook, drawing cook's wages. You been working yourselves down these past two weeks. Thought you could use some good grub. And it'll save us from swapping off on the cookin' chores."

"We don't need another hand," Red said bluntly.

"Hell, Red, you're poor as a crow. You better get on the outside of a few good meals before we hit town, or the women won't even know you." Gunderson grinned at the acerbic wrangler.

"As long as he ain't a full partner, I don't care," Sparky said. "I'll just be glad to turn these edgy critters into cash in a couple o' days."

José said nothing.

If Johnson was a little leery of their suspicious attitude, he didn't show it. Perhaps he was used to dealing with brusque whites.

"Anyway, I'm ramrodding this here outfit, so we got a cook until Ash Fork," Gunderson finished, reining his horse around and riding off into the darkness. The stock of a Winchester protruded from a scabbard behind his leg. Each man was armed with both a long gun and a sidearm, as Gunderson had said. José swung into the saddle and started out at a walk toward the opposite side of the herd they could barely sense nearby in the murk.

Red and Sparky unsaddled and hobbled their horses, then sought their blankets on the edge of the circle of light.

"I hope C.E. doesn't send somebody looking for you, too," Ormond said in an undertone to the black man.

"Anybody come lookin' won't have no trouble spottin' me," Johnson said. "In this country, I blend in like a plum in vanilla pudding."

The night thickened up and the stars disappeared. Ormond, sleeping face down on his Navajo blanket, was awakened by a sprinkle of cold rain. He rolled over and pushed up to one elbow, groaning at his stiffness from sleeping on the hard ground. There was no hint of dawn in the blackness. He had no idea of the time, but felt as if he'd been asleep only a short while. He heard someone stirring, and sensed Johnson nearby, raking over the dampened ashes to find and coax some life from the imbedded coals.

"Hustle up with that grub, Johnson," Gunderson's voice said from the blackness. "We need to be on the move as soon as it's light enough to see."

"Yes, sir."

"You don't have to 'sir' me," the foreman growled. "Just do your job and I'll pay you at the end of the trip. We don't have but about fifty miles to go."

If Gunderson was back from night herd, it was four o'clock or later. Ormond had slept longer than he thought. He rolled over and reached for his boots.

Johnson broke up some small sticks of dry mesquite and fed the tiny flame he'd finally resurrected. Within seconds he had bacon sizzling. From long practice, he was quick and efficient. There was no wasted motion.

Ormond ran a comb through his damp hair and put on his hat as Gunderson was rousing up Red and Sparky. "Shake it outta there," he said in a husky voice. "We got a long way to go today. Grab some coffee and grub." Then in a more relaxed voice: "I believe our new cook has got us a treat this morning."

By the low flicker of flames, Ormond could see the black man turning golden-brown pancakes. "I even bought some maple syrup in town yesterday," the foreman said.

Three-quarters of an hour later, the men had eaten, saddled their mounts, packed their bedrolls, and donned their slickers against the steady drizzle. Dawn was struggling to gray the eastern horizon, but it was not yet light enough to start. The men stood silently, nursing a second or third cup of coffee, water dripping from hat brims as they inclined their heads to sip the black, steaming brew. To stave off weariness from days of grueling work and lack of sleep, they would drain the coffee pot before they mounted up.

Without making a fuss about it, Gunderson saddled Johnson's horse. In the meantime, the cook was scouring the utensils with damp sand and rinsing them in a bucket of water from the nearby Verde River.

"Kick some dirt on that fire and let's go," Gunderson said when the rising sun flashed a narrow streak below the cloud cover on the horizon. A minute later, it was smothered by the overcast, but there was still enough light to see the herd.

Red, the best horseman, rode point, and Sparky and José contained the tired herd on either side. Gunderson rode drag with Johnson and Ormond, mostly to watch their back trail. The light rain dampened any dust and Ormond was grateful for the sandy soil underfoot that kept the ground from becoming slick with mud. There was no thought of stopping for lunch. They would push on to take advantage of all the daylight hours. The horsemen held a steady pace, but allowed the animals to pause and drink now and then from puddles cupped in hollows of ochre-colored rock. A few of the older horses' ribs were visible.

Ormond was becoming accustomed to the stock saddle. He hadn't ridden in months, but by mid-afternoon his previous experience came flooding back. The foreman's well-trained horse was easy to manage.

The herd was still wild, but Gunderson and his wranglers had pushed them hard for several days to make them manageable. Riding behind those bobbing heads and rumps for hours, Ormond was lulled into a hypnotic rhythm. A tilt of the head, a squint of the eyes, a relaxed imagination, and he could see them as the tough little Spanish horses that carried Father Kino and his party through this country some 200 years before. Bloodlines of living history. The buyers would probably preserve and breed them. No dog food or glue factory for these proud descendents.

Just before dark, Gunderson called a halt and the wranglers turned the herd so they were slowly milling at the base of a steeply sloping hillside. A rope corral was quickly improvised with long lariats looping from mesquite to paloverde to any stunted bushes within reach.

"Not secure, but they're probably too tired to get frisky," the foreman said. "If they decide to run all at once, we'd lose 'em, sure. But, unless something scares 'em, they'll be docile enough tonight." He raised his head and sniffed, testing the air. "No lightning or thunder with this rain. It's too cold. Probably snowing in the higher elevations."

"How far you reckon we came today?" Ormond asked, dismounting stiffly.

"About halfway," Gunderson said. "We might get to Ash Fork by tomorrow night, but I don't want to push too hard. They're lean enough as is. But I'll be breathing a lot easier when we collect the cash for them."

"You still think somebody is dogging our trail?" Ormond asked in a low voice. He noticed the foreman hobbling his horse and loosening the cinch, leaving his mount saddled.

"Not sure," he finally answered, "but I'm going to be ready. Didn't see anybody today, but tonight is their last shot at us before we hit town. Of course," he added after a pause, "they might decide to jump us during the day. The sound of gunfire would start the herd running."

"You're convinced, then, that it's not the rancher or a posse?"

"Yep. Any legitimate authority would have ridden right in and braced us long before now. And there ain't any hostile Indians in these parts any more, so that leaves only rustlers and gunmen. Outlaw gangs."

A slight shiver went over Ormond at these words and he moved toward the fire that Johnson was laying. The provident cook had rolled a small bundle of dry sticks into a poncho before the rain soaked everything at last night's campsite. Now the dry kindling was blazing up. The black cook had kept mostly silent since joining the outfit, and the wranglers accepted and ignored him, except at mealtime.

"Wouldn't it be easier and more profitable for outlaws to just rob a bank or a train?" Ormond asked, looking at the foreman, unable to get the idea off his mind that they were being stalked.

"These horses are valuable. Easy pickin's, compared to those other crimes you mentioned."

"Why not rustle cattle, then?"

"Except for a few mavericks or new calves, they're branded, and most of 'em been fenced these later years. Besides, except for a short stampede, cows can't run worth sour apples. Nope. Whoever's out there knows these horses are more valuable than the usual wild mustangs, and they're fixin' to snatch 'em and run to beat hell."

Ormond jerked awake with the sound of a rifle shot ringing in his ears. He rolled away, clawing for his holstered Bisley. The coffee pot had been blasted off the fire and lay hissing among the scattered coals.

"Millard! You OK?"

No answer.

More shots. In the blackness came a shouted warning from Gunderson on night herd, then a growing rumble of galloping hoof beats.

Ormond had his Colt in hand, but could see nothing to fire at. A heavy overcast blotted the stars and moon. Darting muzzle flashes pierced the darkness more than fifty yards away. He shoved the gun back in its holster and fumbled to yank on his damp boots. He heard the two off-watch wranglers curse as they jumped for their hobbled horses that were plunging and whinnying.

"Peter!"

Ormond jumped up, stamping his feet into his boots. "Millard, where are you?" He could hear the black man struggling to throw a saddle on his horse. Ormond went to help, and got the mount ready to ride within a minute, then they turned their attention to Ormond's horse. Meanwhile, sounds of a running battle continued.

"This way!" Ormond yelled. "Somebody's after the herd!"

The two men rode toward the yells and hoof beats. The volume of gunfire indicated the number of attackers far out-numbered their own crew. The rumble of galloping hoofs slowly receded, and Ormond kicked his mount to a run. Suddenly his horse stumbled in the dark, throwing him over his head. Ormond felt himself flying upside down for long, heart-stopping seconds. He crashed through a bush, breaking his fall, before plowing into the wet, sandy soil. Stunned, he lay still for several seconds, trying to get his bearings.

"Peter! You hurt?" Johnson's voice.

"Yeah . . . no." He rolled over, checking himself for in-juries.

The black man materialized out of the gloom. "Can you get up?"

Ormond staggered to his feet and clutched for Johnson's saddle horn to steady himself. "I'll be OK. Where's my horse?"

"He got up and run off."

Ormond heard an approaching rider. Gunderson reined up shortly, nearly running into the pair. "They jumped us and got the herd. Must be at least a dozen of the bastards. They were all over us before we knew what happened."

"Lemme find my horse, and we'll go after 'em," Ormond said.

"Forget the herd. They shot Red. José and Sparky are somewhere out there. But there's several of them on my tail right now." He glanced back into the darkness.

"Why?" Ormond's balance was still off and he couldn't seem to pull his thoughts together.

"They'll try to gun us down so there's nobody left to chase them," Gunderson said. "Jump up behind Johnson, there, and follow me. We have to shake 'em."

Johnson gave him an arm up and Ormond grabbed the black man around the middle as the horse plunged away, nearly unseating him. They could barely keep the foreman in sight as they galloped through the darkness for more than a quarter mile.

Then Gunderson reined up and slid out of the saddle, yanking the Winchester from its scabbard and letting the horse plunge away. "Down behind these boulders!"

Ormond and Johnson followed, just as a shot blasted behind them. The bullet splintered chips of rock near Ormond's hand. He slid down and pulled his Bisley. Gunderson was firing at the muzzle flashes, and Ormond's Bisley was jumping and blazing. Shadowy forms of horses thundered past as the charging horsemen veered away, still shooting. Ormond ducked and held his breath. Then, suddenly, it was quiet. His ears were ringing from the explosions. He let out a long breath, his heart pounding. He could hear water gurgling softly nearby.

"Where the hell are we?" he whispered.

"Limestone Cañon," Gunderson panted. "The Verde River's behind us."

"They're trying to kill us." Ormond couldn't seem to grasp the reality of it.

"No pursuit. No witnesses," Gunderson said, reloading his Winchester.

"The defenders have become the hunted."

"Can you handle a pistol?" Gunderson asked Johnson, who lay wedged between them.

"Yes."

Gunderson handed his Colt to Johnson.

Ormond began reloading. "I can't hear the herd."

"They ran 'em off southeast, toward Cottonwood. Those yahoos were ready and outnumbered us at least three to one. They let us do most of the work trailing the herd, then just rode in and took 'em. Damn! Cut the rope corral and spooked 'em with gunfire. Once they started running, me and Red couldn't turn 'em. Then those riders opened up on us."

"We'd best be lookin' to our own safety," Ormond said. "How long till daylight?"

"Hours."

"Now that we're afoot, do you think they'll wait until dawn to pick us off?"

"Don't know. But darkness is our friend. Let's move out of here in case they come back." Gunderson rocked to his feet, trailing the Winchester as he started off at a half jog.

"You know this area?" Ormond asked in a stage whisper as he scrambled to follow. Johnson was right on his heels.

"Sort of."

They stopped talking and stumbled along single file.

"Hold it." They hunkered down, panting, and listened intently. The sound of horsemen coming closer. The unseen riders paused, and Ormond could hear mumbled voices. Then the hoof beats began to recede.

The three men moved on, their footfalls nearly soundless on the wet sand. The rain had stopped, but Ormond was soaked with sweat and from brushing against wet desert shrubs. He heard Gunderson curse softly as he stumbled up a steep incline. A few seconds later the three of them stood atop a railroad embankment.

"Now I know where I am," Gunderson said. "That light about a mile up yonder is the Limestone Cañon depot. Let's go."

"Look!" Johnson was pointing behind them. The headlight of a train coming from the south. They stood and watched it approach for a long minute until they could begin to hear the *chuffing* of the locomotive. It seemed to be moving at less than twenty miles an hour.

"Our salvation," Gunderson said, throwing the carbine into the crook of his arm.

A handgun blasted in the darkness behind them and a bullet whanged off the iron rail near their feet. All three instinctively dropped down the other side of the embankment. Gunderson fired off three quick rifle shots in the general direction of their pursuers. They heard the sound of galloping horses as the attackers rode parallel to the right of way, just out of sight across the tracks. Then two horsemen rode up to the top of the embankment within fifty yards of the approaching train. The steam whistle wailed its warning. Before the attackers could ride down out of the headlight beam, Gunderson fired. One man toppled off down the slope, and the other man came charging his mount down into the darkness toward them. Johnson and Ormond both fired, guessing where the gunman was. Ormond could hear nothing over the sound of gunfire and the train whistle. The locomotive was rearing up, nearly on them.

"Come on!" Gunderson shouted at the last second, and the three men scrambled up and darted across the tracks only a few feet in front of the slow-moving cowcatcher. The iron monster rumbled past, effectively blocking off the attacker on the other side.

"Get aboard!" Gunderson ran along the uneven roadbed, stumbling, and flung his rifle onto the platform between two of the lighted passenger coaches. Two men, standing outside, smoking, reached down to grab and pull him aboard.

Ormond and Johnson got a later start and had to run for

the next car. But the train was slowing for the depot and water tank ahead, so it was rolling only about ten miles an hour. Ormond holstered his Colt, watching for a chance. Jogging alongside, Johnson first, then Ormond, grabbed the iron railing and jumped onto the steps, leaving their pursuer in the darkness behind.

Chapter Five

"You boys could 'a' waited till we stopped at the depot," a man in a blue military tunic said, eyeing the three disheveled strangers who'd suddenly appeared in the crowded passenger car.

"And let somebody get ahead of us?" Gunderson blustered. "Hell, no!"

Ormond said nothing, trying to figure out what they had jumped into. About half of the forty-odd men in the car were munching sandwiches and pickles and swigging beer from bottles. A layer of blue smoke drifted past the chandeliers toward the overhead ventilators while men puffed on corncob pipes. Some kind of private party, maybe. Ormond rubbed his eyes. Odd—no women were present. He recalled the patriotic bunting on the outside of the coach. Was this a military train? Not likely, since no one was in uniform except the man who'd addressed them, and he was wearing lieutenant's bars on his shoulders.

Ormond and Johnson looked to Gunderson to take the lead in bluffing their way into this group. Obviously this was not the average public conveyance.

Gunderson had his Winchester in hand; Ormond his

holstered Bisley, while Johnson had shoved Gunderson's Colt under his belt. The three were wet and grimy and smelled of spent gunpowder. Gunderson was the only one of them who still had his hat.

The train slowed and Ormond staggered forward, off balance, catching the back of a seat to steady himself.

"Well, if you boys are that eager to sign up, we'll take you," the lieutenant continued. "It may throw us over our quota, but we'll have a few fall out along the way. Give Sergeant Macklin your names and where you're from. Of course, this is only conditional on you passing your physicals later when the doc can get to you. You'll be formally mustered and assigned a troop when we get to San Antonio."

A lean, hard-looking man with a drooping mustache—apparently Sergeant Macklin—put down a hunk of yellow cheese he was chewing on, and picked up a pad and pencil.

One by one the trio gave their names and ages, and their place of residence as Flagstaff.

"You're a mite old for active military duty, ain't ya, pap?" The sergeant looked hard at Millard Johnson when he gave his age as fifty-one.

"I'm strong for my age," Johnson replied.

"He can be assigned to the buffalo soldiers of the Tenth Cavalry," the lieutenant said.

"No bedrolls? No luggage?" the sergeant inquired.

"Nope. We were in a hurry. Afraid we'd miss ya," Gunderson replied quickly for all of them.

"Well, I'll see if the acting quartermaster can rustle up some blankets. We got four coaches on this train. I don't think the last one is quite full. There's some pigs' feet, boiled ham, bread and stuff. Get yourselves something to eat, and settle in. You can hunker down by the stove back there and get dried off."

"Thanks, Sarge," Gunderson said, motioning for Ormond and Johnson to retreat. The pair followed the raw-boned foreman out the end door, crossed through the next car, and found themselves on the deserted rear platform. The train pulled no caboose.

"What've we got ourselves into?" Ormond asked, when they were alone in the dark.

The train ground to a halt at the tiny wooden depot and water tower.

Gunderson moved to one side to avoid being silhouetted in the light coming from the window in the end door. "I shot one of them two," he said, staring off into the darkness behind the train. "The other one might still be on our tail."

"Oh, he's probably discouraged by now and took off to catch up with his friends and the herd," Ormond said.

"That kind of thinking has got many a man killed," Gunderson replied in a low voice. "They seemed pretty determined to leave no one to chase them."

"So, what now?" Johnson asked.

"This has to be a special train for the Arizona Volunteer Regiment that formed up at Whipple Barracks in Prescott," Gunderson said.

"What?"

"Peter, you've got to start reading the newspapers and keeping up with what's going on in the world." Gunderson pushed his hat back. "The United States has declared war."

"I heard. And you think this is the bunch from Whipple Barracks?"

"Our troops are off to fight the Spanish in Cuba. And, like it or not, we've just signed up for it."

They stood silently, absorbing this new state of affairs.

The sounds of voices from up ahead came faintly to their ears as the crew scurried to take on water for the panting locomotive.

"We can slip off in the dark at Ash Fork or Flagstaff," Johnson suggested.

Neither man responded immediately. Finally Gunderson spoke. "I've lost my herd, my wranglers, both my horses and gear. Damned if I don't feel like taking it out on those arrogant Spanish bastards I've been reading about who've been beating up on poor Cubans, strip-searching women for contraband, and all that."

"You mean you want to stay in this volunteer outfit?" Ormond asked.

"What else have I got?"

Another silence.

"Well, I've lost most of the old man's coins, resigned my job, lost out on the money from those Spanish horses. I guess my next occupation will be that of a soldier," Ormond said, sizing up his prospects.

"I got me twelve of C.E.'s coins, but I can't go back with just those," Johnson said. "The old man would have me arrested, for sure."

"You're staying with us?"

"Appears so, if they don't reject me for being too old."

"Worse comes to worst, every commissary needs a good cook," Gunderson said.

"Better than being shot at, anyway," Ormond added.

"Looks like it's settled," Gunderson said.

The blast of a steam whistle sounded and the train jerked into motion. The depot, lighted by a single hurricane lantern, slid past into the blackness.

"Let's get those blankets and something to eat," Gunderson said. He paused with his hand on the door handle. "I'm a fair judge of men," he mused. "I had a hunch those three buyers I lined up through the Breeders' Association were a shifty, underhanded lot. They wouldn't advance me any expense money to get the horses, but I figured they didn't trust me. Turns out, I shouldn't have trusted them, just because they were wearing white shirts and ties. Now, I ain't so sure but what they didn't send some riders to steal that herd so they didn't have to pay for 'em."

"That's kinda far-fetched thinking."

"No. We rounded up the horses down by the border, trailed them almost to Ash Fork, and wore them down a good deal, then those rustlers picked a remote spot to kill us and steal the herd. At the time I wondered why those buyers didn't arrange to meet us in Tucson and load the horses on the train there. It would have been a lot easier. But they had something else in mind."

"If you believe that's what happened, why don't we drop off in Ash Fork and go after them? We could get the law involved. Maybe find Sparky and Red and José," Ormond said.

Gunderson shook his head. "At the next stop I'll fire off a telegram to the Yavapai County sheriff back in Prescott, for whatever good it'll do. But you can bet that herd's gone. It was all too well planned. Those rustlers were trailing us for days." He opened the door to the combination baggage car. "I've joined up and I'll see it through, come what may. I hope both of you will stick, too."

"We'll get the lieutenant to assign us to the same troop."

In spite of what Sergeant Macklin had said about vacant seats, the three men finally appropriated some space in the baggage car atop the mail pouches. "A darn' sight more comfortable than being jackknifed into those day coach seats," Gunderson remarked as they rolled into their blankets.

They were just beginning to relax and doze when the train rolled into the mainline junction at Ash Fork to an enthusiastic celebration. The shouting, flag-waving townspeople crowded the depot platform to cheer the 200 volunteers who filed off the Santa Fe, Prescott, and Phoenix special and crossed the tracks to board the cars of the eastbound Santa Fe Pacific. The locomotive was waiting with steam up.

" 'Boooooarrrd!" The conductor waved his lantern to signal the engineer and swung onto the step as the train began to move.

But the passengers got little sleep. The train reached the 7,000-foot elevation of Flagstaff at 2:30 a.m. in the midst of a heavy snowfall. But that didn't dampen the spirits of the throng that greeted them with cheers and banners reading **Remember the Maine** and **The Arizona Cowboy Regiment**.

Hoary Civil War veterans, proudly wearing remnants of their uniforms and medals, hurrahed and waved, tears in their eyes. Children, who'd been kept awake or rousted out of bed, stood with their parents. Men and women of all ages clapped and shouted, waving a sea of white handkerchiefs.

"I didn't figure *anything* could beat the send-off by the territorial governor in Prescott," one volunteer remarked, looking through the car window. "But these folks just came out to see *us*."

"You'd think we were already returning heroes, instead of just going off to war," Ormond said when the train began to pull away.

All along the route, this scene was repeated—proud citi-

74

zens vying with each other to show support for the volunteers, crowding up to shake hands through the open train windows, touching the men, trying to slap their backs, shouting good wishes, pressing good luck charms into their hands.

At Albuquerque the next day, they changed trains again, this time to the Southern Pacific. Several of the more competitive members of the contingent went to Western Union in the depot to telegraph a message to the New Mexico volunteers who were gathering at Las Vegas. A man named John Murphy reëntered the coach, waving a copy of the message. "Listen to this, boys!" he shouted. "This'll get their goat . . . 'Roosevelt's Troopers, Santa Fe. Isleta, N.M., May 6 . . . What the hell matter with New Mexico? Come running or will never get to Cuba. Brodie's Arizonians, two hundred strong.' "

"*Whew!* That oughta fetch 'em!" another man whooped. "But we'll still be the first to San Antone!"

In all, the trip from Prescott to San Antonio took sixty hours. Between sleeping and eating and responding to cheering crowds, the three late volunteers agreed that the trip did not seem long or dull or tiring. However, being jackknifed into the seats of the day coaches was not conducive to sleep.

"Even these Texans who have Southern sympathies are turning out to cheer us," Ormond remarked.

"We're off to fight the Spanish devils," Gunderson said. "The country hasn't had a war since you and I were colts."

"I wasn't even old enough for the last one," Johnson observed, striking a match to his stubby briar. "One o' my uncles was in a colored regiment for the Union."

"I'm ready for a bath," Ormond said. "I believe I could enjoy train travel, but I'd want it to be on a transcontinental express in a plush Pullman with most of my meals in a diner . . . not a week in a day coach with a scruffy bunch of men who haven't bathed or shaved."

"Let's hope Army life is better," Gunderson said.

"Don't bet on it," Johnson said.

"You always expect the worst," Ormond remarked.

"I seen a lot more summers than you boys. If a man brace up for the worst, and it don't happen, then he feels mighty proud. That's the way I see it, 'specially those years I work for yo Daddy," he added.

"Don't know how you stood it," Ormond marveled.

"A man does what a man has to do," Johnson replied simply, puffing on his pipe.

On the dreary, hot stretch across Texas they were careful to avoid Florence, a feisty mountain lion cub that had been donated as a mascot by a Prescott saloonkeeper. The animal roamed freely in the baggage car and was fed a variety of strange foods, but seemed to adjust well to all the human turmoil.

At El Paso, a comely Negro girl volunteered to come aboard for the rest of the trip—to the cheers of most of the men. But the officers quickly squelched that plan.

Ormond was only half awake before dawn on May 2nd when the special train rolled into San Antonio.

Colonel Leonard Wood, who commanded the volunteer forces from the Territories, had arranged for their arrival, and they were hurried off the train, grimy and bewhiskered, to board the Edison Line streetcars. In the chilly, graying dawn they rode three miles south from the city to a 600-acre fairground site that was enclosed by a high board fence.

"Welcome to Riverside Park, now known as Camp Wood!" one of the officers announced as he stepped off the streetcar and waited for the men to stream out behind him. "Stow your gear on the floor of that big building over there . . . the exhibition hall. The cooks have a hot breakfast waiting for you."

"Wonder what the Army got to eat?" Johnson said as the three men headed toward the hall. They had no gear, so made directly for the tables and the delicious smells of frying bacon.

"A man has to be flexible," Ormond replied. "I'll let myself be herded toward free food."

"I've a hunch you won't think it's free by the time we're done here," Gunderson predicted.

That afternoon, the three men were officially mustered in. Ormond was assigned to C Troop, led by Captain Joseph Alexander, a former regular Army officer. In spite of his request to be assigned to A Troop, officered by Bucky O'Neill, Irish-born mayor of Prescott, Gunderson was also assigned to C Troop.

"But I just came from Prescott," Gunderson argued.

"Don't matter. That's where our train started from and most of us joined up at Whipple Barracks," the sergeant said, entering Gunderson's name in the big ledger on the table before him. "Might near every man here would like to be in Bucky's outfit, but it can't be. So that's that." He looked up. "Next!"

Johnson stepped up. "Millard Johnson, sir."

The grizzled sergeant looked him up and down. "You only say 'sir' to officers. Johnson, is it? You must be even older than I am, 'cause you colored folks don't show your age much."

"Close to fifty, Sergeant."

"*Hmmm* . . . don't know your birth date, I guess. On the high side of fifty-five, I'd say. The Tenth is all colored, but they're regular Army, not volunteers. B'sides, they don't take recruits your age."

Just then an officer walked behind the table, saw Johnson, and paused.

"Occupation?" the sergeant inquired.

"Servant."

"In a restaurant?"

"I. . . ."

"If he knows his way around a kitchen, put him in the commissary unit," the officer interrupted.

"No, sir, I. . . ."

"Don't argue, man. You'll go where you're assigned, or you won't go at all."

"The commissariat it is, sir," the sergeant said, apparently relieved to have this decision taken out of his hands. "The doctor will examine you this afternoon," he added to the volunteers.

"Don't worry, Millard, this is probably for the best," Ormond said. They walked out into the sunshine toward the headquarters tent of C Troop.

"I'd best report in, then," Johnson said, mopping his shining face with a bandanna. "The kitchen's in the back of the exhibition hall."

"See you later," Ormond said. He could also feel sweat trickling down his nose and the back of his neck.

"Makes a man wish for some of that Flagstaff snow," Gunderson remarked. "It must be at least ninety humid degrees here."

"South Texas was never known for cold weather in May," Ormond said.

He gripped Johnson's hand, and they parted. On their trip from the territory, Ormond had grown fond of the old servant. If the man possessed anything in abundance, it was durability and patience. He would roll with whatever came, and survive.

They reported to the big, white headquarters tent where a man in shirt sleeves sat at a small folding table under the tent fly.

"Pick you a comfortable spot on the floor of the exhibition hall until some shelter halves and bedrolls arrive from Fort Sam Houston," the man told them as he logged their names onto the company roster. "Probably be a few days before the rest of your gear gets here by train from Eastern warehouses. By the way, I'm First Sergeant Willis Huson. Welcome to C Troop. After you have your physicals, you're on your own until tomorrow morning. The Arizona Rough Riders were the first to arrive, so it'll be a while before everything starts to shake down."

Rough Riders? Ormond raised his eyebrows. Maybe word of his lack of riding skill had somehow preceded him.

"That's what the San Antonio papers have been calling us for a week," the sergeant said. "Has a nice ring to it, don't you think?" He grinned. The man had a neatly trimmed mustache and pomaded dark hair. He looked like a clerk, but Ormond was to learn later that Huson was a lawyer from Yuma.

After a cursory physical exam, Gunderson and Ormond rode the trolley into town and spent the rest of the afternoon walking and looking. They cooled off with a couple of chilled beers in a shady, open-air saloon before returning to the fairgrounds, or to Camp Wood, as the sentry at the gate reminded them. A high wooden fence surrounded the 600-acre park.

They looked for Johnson at supper, half expecting him to be on the serving line. But he'd already been assigned to cooking duties. They saw him sweating by one of the giant ranges in the back of the big building. The doors stood open, but the sluggish outside air was not making inroads into the heat that hung near the high ceiling of the exhibition hall and the 100-plus-degree temperature in the vicinity of the cooking food.

Next day, a supply of tents arrived and Ormond and Gunderson were on hand to claim two of the white shelter halves as they were unloaded near the rail siding. There were not enough to go around, but at least they'd gotten one of the first and erected it per instructions at the beginning of a neat row. They were glad to be off the hard floor of the exhibition hall where noisy boots clumped in and out at all hours. At least now they had a little privacy, a blanket each, and the benefit of any cooler night air.

The following afternoon, 340 volunteers from New Mexico Territory unloaded from a special twelve-car train. The contingent of eighty-three from Oklahoma joined the Arizonans in giving their newly arrived comrades a lusty cheer as they marched in a double column through the wide gate.

A small group of Easterners, many from colleges in New England, arrived that day on their own. Although the volunteers were supposed to hail from the Territories, the authorized strength of the regiment had been increased from 780 to 1,000, leaving room for extra volunteers, mostly young athletes and sportsmen from well-to-do families in the East. Nearly all of them were personal friends of Lieutenant Colonel Theodore Roosevelt, second in command under Colonel Leonard Wood.

A week later, First Lieutenant Allyn Capron, on detached service from the 7th Cavalry, brought in 170 troopers from the Indian Territory, virtually completing the number of the 1st Volunteer Cavalry, now quickly being recognized as the Rough Riders in everything except official correspondence.

By the time the regiment was nearly up to strength, the men had been drilling for several days. They still wore civilian clothes and were using brooms for rifles as the sergeants put them through close order drill and instructed them in the manual of arms. "Right front into line!" "Fours right about!" "Right by file!"—commands that had not changed since the Civil War. Straw boaters, stiff collars, and patent leather shoes marched alongside blue denim overalls and work shoes and chaps, felt hats and spurred boots. In spite of the fact that there were horses in the camp, and more arriving every day, all their marching was done afoot.

"I thought this was a cavalry outfit," Gunderson grumbled to Ormond as they marched in step in column formation. "These damned boots of mine were never made for this."

"Starting with the basics," Ormond replied. He realized everyone was learning to listen for and obey commands and to work in squads and platoons, then in company formation. The commands would vary when the volunteers graduated to the mounted cavalry. But for now they endured many hours of drill in the basic infantry movements. From reading Civil War stories, Ormond knew that the stress of actual battle would negate most of these maneuvers anyway. Finally uniforms and gear began to trickle in. All of it was off-loaded from baggage and boxcars, and dispensed by sweating sergeants according to seniority, giving the Arizona men first choice.

As civilian clothes were shed, a few used clothing dealers from San Antonio were standing by, hoping to pick up bargains. They were on hand every time new uniforms were distributed. One wiry man with a Roman nose out of all proportion to his face stepped up and held out a shiny quarter. "Twenty-five cents for your old suit!" he chirped to a man who was drawing his uniform. The volunteer paused and looked down at the suit he was wearing. "This suit cost me thirty dollars in Phoenix two months ago," he said. "And there's not a mark on it." He exchanged a knowing look with several of his nearby friends. They silently nodded, then rushed for the merchant, pinning his arms. Two others produced a blanket and the merchant was tossed down on it while four brawny men took the corners. "One . . . two . . . *three!*" The blanket was heaved up and the man flung into the air. He yelled in terror as he came down, was caught, and tossed again, higher. He flailed his arms and legs, trying to keep from falling on his head.

This continued for two minutes until they grew tired and let the little merchant go. "And don't come back, ya cheatin' little weasel!" a man jeered at the disheveled victim who staggered away toward the gate, leaving his crushed bowler on the ground behind him.

Gunderson had to exchange his khaki canvas trousers with another man for a longer pair that fit. He and Ormond each drew the standard issue cheap cotton underwear, socks, rugged, high-topped shoes, tough canvas leggings, a heavy blue flannel shirt, trousers and jacket of brown canvas, topped by a gray campaign hat. One man, who had served a hitch in the cavalry, held up the jacket and trousers. "This looks like the uniform I wore to shovel out the stables!"

"That's what they are!" a sergeant behind the long table snapped. "When Colonel Wood was chasing Geronimo around in Mexico, he found out these work better as a duty uniform. Cooler, and they don't tear up as quick in the brush."

Favorable comments filled the air as each man was issued a single-action Colt .45 and a bolt-action Krag carbine. Gunderson still had his own Colt and Winchester, and Ormond his new nickel-plated Bisley .32-20, but they accepted the standard weapons anyway.

"I'll sell my personal guns in town tomorrow," Gunderson decided. They stowed uniforms and the new weapons securely under blankets in their tent, then went back for their horse gear. Each man received a McClellan saddle.

"You need about a fourteen-inch seat," the supply sergeant estimated, eyeing Gunderson's big-boned frame. "And you'll take a twelve," he said, heaving the slotted saddle at Ormond. The seat size was stamped into a small brass shield affixed to the pommel. As the men moved down the line, the remainder of their gear was piled, piece by piece, atop the saddles they cradled—rifle boot, saddlebags, grooming kit, surcingle, latigo cinch straps, halter shank, saddle blanket, browbands and headstalls tangled together. Much of this leather gear was dusty and dry, right out of storage, but other pieces appeared well used and still oiled.

"Gonna take a lot of saddle soap and elbow grease to get some of this stuff ready to use," Gunderson remarked as they lugged the pile to their tent.

But, over the next few days, it was accomplished. The volunteers, in uniform, now began to look as if they belonged together.

Lieutenant Colonel Theodore Roosevelt considered the 1st Volunteer Cavalry his own personal fighting force. He made a point to meet each man, shake his hand, ask a few questions about his background, and give him a blue polka dot bandanna that he'd decided would be the trademark of the Rough Riders. He told them it should be worn with pride to distinguish themselves from all other troops that would be gathering in Florida for transport to Cuba.

As Roosevelt passed along their mess table, it was Ormond's first chance to get a good look at their commander. He had the informality of a volunteer soldier, but Ormond decided it was just the man's effusive personality that endeared him to his subordinates. He had the enthusiasm of a boy. This was his war; he had pushed for it in speeches and political maneuvering as Assistant Secretary of the Navy. And now he was here to lead his own volunteers into battle. Apparently Colonel Leonard Wood had given him much latitude.

"Thank you, Colonel," Ormond said, hurriedly wiping his mouth and twisting away from the table to accept the polka dot bandanna. "Blue and white are my favorite colors."

"Where are you from, son?" Roosevelt asked.

"Prescott, sir."

"Then you know Captain O'Neill! Good man!"

"Not personally, sir." He stood up and gripped Roosevelt's hand. At five-foot ten, he was some taller than this bull-necked man in his tailor-made khaki uniform. The commander was built like a barrel, but his most obvious features were his big, white teeth, showing in a perpetual grin beneath his mustache, and his round, steel-rimmed spectacles.

As Roosevelt moved down the table, Ormond recalled how several of the men had been contemptuous of Roosevelt at first, labeling him a rich, over-age dude, here to play at soldiering. But they quickly warmed to his genuine enthusiasm. Ormond knew this man was no Eastern dilettante. By sheer will power and effort he'd overcome a sickly childhood to become an athlete in college. Following the deaths of his wife and mother in the 1880s, he'd gone West to start a ranch in the wilds of North Dakota. He was familiar with all kinds of guns and hunted big game. He'd even chased, captured, and brought to justice several frontier thieves.

Gunderson knotted the blue polka dot bandanna around his neck. "If anyone can make this war as exciting and fun as a football match, he's the one," he remarked, picking up his fork.

"He reminds me of a coach."

Almost by mutual consent, the volunteers decided to outfit each company with a distinctive color of horse, a tradition in past cavalry units. So began much swapping, some of it accomplished at night from picket lines. A few Eastern dudes brought their own horses, and an expensive polo pony turned up missing until its owner tracked it down in another company. O'Neill's troop chose bays, Captain McClintock's, sorrels, and the men of Captain Alexander's C Troop decided on dappled grays.

The horses had been purchased locally by the remount service and gathered at Fort Sam Houston. Wranglers drove them to Camp Wood. In theory, each of these horses qualified for the military according to standards of the regular cavalry. Each was to be at least four years old, sound of limb and wind, fifteen or more hands high, and weigh approximately 1,100 to 1,250 pounds. Another requirement was circumvented. Each animal was supposed to have been saddled and ridden. Some of them had never had a saddle on their backs.

The genuine cowboys in the regiment, such as Sam

Rhodes of the Tonto Basin and Frank Van Siclin of Safford, and others, enjoyed riding these unbroken horses. A lot of wagering went on among them and their backers as to who could stick the longest to the backs of these bucking broncos. In addition, the cowboys accepted the standard $10 fee to break mounts for the less experienced riders. Fortunately Ormond was able to rely on Gunderson to procure two manageable horses for both of them.

The sweltering days passed and Ormond met many other volunteers, including A Troop's Charles Hodgdon, universally referred to as "Happy Jack" for his constant smile and clownish antics. Another A Troop man, Daniel Hogan of Flagstaff, became known as the "Admiral of the Hassayamp" from his habit of entertaining Eastern dudes with hair-raising tall tales of boating on the Hassayampa River. All the Arizona boys knew that the Hassayampa, which originated in the mountains near Prescott and flowed into the Gila west of Phoenix, contained water only after a heavy rain or snowfall.

Another man, a boisterous hell-raiser, became "Prayerful James" to his fellow troopers. Charles Younger, a fireman from Winslow, reportedly was a cousin of the infamous Younger brothers.

Gunderson had truthfully given his previous occupation as ranch foreman, while Ormond had signed on as clerk, his most recent job. Truthful or not, the two men met many others who claimed to be everything—insurance agent, miner, bookkeeper, engineer, salesman, painter, prospector, rancher, cowboy. They were as diverse a group of men as Ormond could possibly imagine. Most were in their twenties, but a good number, like Ormond and Gunderson, were past thirty. Several claimed foreign birth in England, Ireland, Switzerland, or Scotland.

The men of each company named the street that divided their rows of tents. Troop A named theirs O'Neill Avenue for their popular commander. The Troop B street became Arizona Avenue. Alexander's Troop C called theirs Manila Avenue.

On May 23rd, the regiment first drilled as a unit. By then, all troopers had been issued carbines and revolvers. On this day, selected troopers with blank cartridges galloped around the regiment, firing their pistols to teach the horses to stand the noise of gunfire. Some stood it well, but most of the untried mounts bucked, or laid back their ears and reared, pawing the air and throwing their riders. Others tried to run.

Ormond's horse began crow-hopping and Ormond managed to stay in the saddle by grabbing the pommel, cursing the fact that the McClellan had no saddle horn to grip in a panic. Even though the hard saddletree was of seasoned hickory covered with a layer of rawhide and one of leather, the deep, narrow seat cupped him comfortably and he found it easier to ride than a stock saddle. He managed to get his mount under control before many of the others. By the time the training was over and the scattered troopers back astride and in formation, Ormond felt he had done rather well. In all the commotion, Gunderson even gave him a grin and a thumbs-up sign.

Chapter Six

During the last week of May, Colonel Wood ordered a substantial increase in drill. This was taken as a sign they were about to receive their marching orders. To get a jump on the heat, drill was called an hour before sunrise; afterwards, the men were kept busy until sunset, with cavalry drill occupying at least six hours a day. Care of the horses, guard mount, manual of arms, target practice, cleaning of weapons, and meals filled the rest of the waking hours.

Firing the Krag carbine was a revelation to Ormond. The first time on the range, he wasn't gripping the weapon and the recoil slammed the steel butt plate into his shoulder. Next time, he was more cautious. The working of the bolt was oily smooth, and the long, bottle-shaped .30-caliber cartridge exploded with an ear-ringing blast. Very much of this would damage his hearing, but it was better than being on the muzzle end of one of these powerful weapons. Targets of muskmelons and watermelons were set up at distances of 100, 200, and 400 yards. He was impressed with the power and accuracy of the hits, from either the prone, the kneeling, or the off-hand positions.

The firing along the line stuttered to a halt as magazines were emptied.

"Hold fire! Any of you who missed, charge downrange and go after them!"

Several of the soldiers turned questioning looks in the sergeant's direction.

"I mean, right now! Git! If you can't hit 'em with a bullet, hit 'em with the butt of your weapon!"

Several soldiers jumped and, yelling fiercely, ran toward the few intact melons on the crates. Reaching the mock enemy, they attacked and burst the melons with the heavy stocks of their Krags.

"That is the Spanish enemy!" the sergeant bellowed, his voice cracking with the strain. "Those are the barbaric bastards who strip-search decent women aboard ship, who starve children, who use slave labor to cut their cane. Remember the *Maine* and those American lives!"

Ormond, who'd hit his target, knelt on one knee and placed his hot Krag on the ground. He looked over at Gunderson.

"I'd hate to be charging into hand-to-hand combat without at least a bayonet," the big man muttered out of the corner of his mouth. Ormond nodded. He wondered why the barrel of the Krag-Jorgensen carbine wasn't designed to accept a bayonet as was the longer rifle version. Then it became obvious—the shorter weapon was meant to be used from horseback by cavalry.

"Kill! Kill!" The red-faced sergeant strode up and down behind the firing line, shouting at the men downrange who were too far away to hear.

Ormond stared silently at Gunderson, wondering what the big man was thinking. The *Insurrectos,* those Cuban nationals who were fighting a rag-tag guerrilla war against the dominant Spanish, obviously needed American help. But for Ormond it would take more than a frenetic sergeant to whip up hatred of a foe he'd never seen. Even the Hearst newspapers, which he seldom read, screamed louder than necessary for Spanish blood. Possibly when he got to Cuba. . . .

"We can thank Colonel Wood and Theodore Roosevelt for these rifles," Gunderson said as they retired from the range to clean the weapons. "The first smokeless repeaters the U.S. Army has ever used. Maybe they'll be a match for the Spanish Mausers."

"I hope so. Knowing our government, there won't be enough of these to go around. But Roosevelt will pull strings and exert pressure where it counts to make sure his Rough Riders are equipped with the latest and best. You can bet the other volunteer companies will be using the old single shot, black powder Springfields that haven't changed since the Civil War."

"You don't have much faith in the military," Gunderson observed. "How do you know all that without ever being on active duty?"

"I've got the sight of my eyes and can hear. Just because I don't often read the paper, doesn't mean I'm entirely ignorant of what's been going on over the years."

Sunday was a day of rest and all drill was suspended. Ormond and Gunderson usually attended the Episcopal Mass, conducted by Chaplain Brown. Later, along with the other soldiers, they boiled their clothes to kill body lice, then spent the rest of the day lounging, napping, and reading. With no one to write to, they saved time on letter writing.

One Sunday afternoon in late May, they managed to slip Millard Johnson away from his duties as cook. The black man looked leaner, his cheek bones a little more prominent.

"Been sweatin' it off," he replied to their queries. "Can't eat much in this heat, or I feel sick. But I feel good," he hastened to assure them. "Gettin' back to my fightin' weight." He grinned, striking a boxer's pose.

The three men wandered away from camp and down under some shade trees toward the back side of the compound. It felt good to get away from the sights and sounds of other soldiers and the crowds of brightly dressed townspeople, swarming into the camp every Sunday to visit, talk with the volunteers, and take pictures with their small Kodaks.

"Are you sorry you came along?" Ormond asked Johnson.

"Not so's you could notice it," Johnson replied, producing a pipe from his pocket and stuffing it with tobacco. Wide galluses supported his regulation canvas pants, and he wore a light cotton shirt, open in front to expose his torso to any vagrant breeze. "C.E., he made me feel low and mean all the time, so I got used to takin' rough orders. But everybody here treats me better than your pappy."

Ormond glanced around. "Still got those coins?" he asked in a lower voice.

"Sure do. I slit a leather belt and sewed 'em inside. And I don't never take that belt off."

"Somebody might notice it and steal it while you're asleep," Gunderson said.

"No. It don't look like no money belt. Besides, it hardly shows next to my skin, and I keep me a sheath knife hanging on it, so anybody'd think I wore it at night just for protection."

"Good thinking," Ormond said. "And, speaking of protection, here's the Colt Forty-Five I was issued. I don't need it. Got my own Bisley and bought a couple boxes of

Thirty-Two cartridges in town."

"Right kind of you," Johnson said, grasping the walnut grip and inspecting the pistol. It was the artillery model with a 5½-inch barrel. Johnson thrust it inside his waistband and put the handful of cartridges into his pocket. He picked up the pipe he'd laid aside, and struck a match to the bowl, puffing it to life.

The men strolled deeper into the woods. Some grass grew thinly in the shade, but there was no underbrush in this park. Coming around the base of a thick oak, Ormond nearly tripped over the legs of a man sprawled out. The sleeper stirred.

"Sorry, mister. Didn't mean to disturb you."

"Quite all right," the stranger said, getting to his feet. He was of average height, but his clean-shaven face emphasized a lean, ascetic appearance. Brown hair was curling at the collar of his white shirt. He could have been anywhere from thirty-five to forty-five years old. "I needed to wake up, anyway. About to drown in my own sweat." He wiped a sleeve across his eyes, then spat to one side.

"It sho' powerful hot," Johnson affirmed.

The man hitched up the rawhide shoulder strap that carried a satchel of some sort. Since he seemed in no hurry to move off, Ormond quickly introduced the three of them.

"Pleased to meet you," the lean stranger said, shaking their hands in turn. He had a slim, but strong grip. "Name's Dismas Saint Cyril. I'm covering all this hoopla for the Chicago *Evening Journal.*"

"Then you're competing with the Hearst papers?"

He nodded. "Most people don't recognize the difference. To them, a newspaper is just a newspaper. Sometimes a man will do damned near anything for his daily bread. But

I wouldn't work for Hearst at any price. I may be a hireling, but I still have *some* principles left." He gave a sardonic grin. "I don't make policy or give opinions. I'm not required to slant my articles or make them sensational . . . I just write facts, paint word pictures, and sometimes send in a few sketches."

"You sound as if you don't have any allegiance to your employer."

"I'm faithful to my duties," St. Cyril responded. "I sold my talent and my services . . . not my soul."

"Well said," Ormond commented.

St. Cyril reached under his vest and drew a slim cigar from his shirt pocket. "Anybody got a match?"

Johnson struck a stick match, and lit the smoke for him.

"Thank you." The reporter took a couple of puffs, then held out the cigar and gave it a critical look. "About half soaked with sweat. I'm surprised it even burns." He took another puff and squinted through the smoke. "You're wearing the blue polka dot neckerchiefs of the Rough Riders," he observed. Then, glancing at Johnson's open white shirt and khaki pants with no leggings, he asked: "What outfit are you with?"

"I'm a cook."

St. Cyril's face lit up. "A real, honest-to-God cook? My hat's off to you, my man, if you can practice your art under these conditions."

Ormond noted this reporter was the first one who'd made no mention of Johnson's age.

"He's good," Gunderson said. "He's been promising us an apple pie. But I guess that's out of the question for now, unless somebody higher up puts it on the menu for the entire mess."

" 'Cepten for the long hours in the heat, it ain't a bad

job. You seen the Buzzacot oven?"

"No. What's that?"

"Army field oven. I been on this earth 'bout twice as long as most men in this camp, and I ain't never laid eyes on the like of it," Johnson declared with awe. "When you gets a chance, take a good, close look at it. Better yet, watch me and the two other cooks operate it. It's a whole passel o' pots and pans . . . big pots and pans . . . of different sizes made to nest right inside each other. Then they's all folded inside two sections of iron grill to make the whole rig portable." He gestured with his hands. "It's a marvel. Burns fuel like a blast furnace. I've more'n likely been toasted a few shades darker from just standing in front of it. And I ain't come close to mastering it yet. Got to learn to bank the coals just so. Once we get it outside, they tell me we got to calculate the wind, too."

"That thing sounds big enough to cook for at least a hundred men at a time," Ormond said.

"More than that. But it takes practice. You got to learn when to shovel big, fat coals onto the lid of a pan to get the heat down on the top side of your roast or beans." He shook his head. "*Whew!* I thought I knew a thing or two about cookin', but I'm just a raw recruit on that Buzzacot."

"I like the wash boiler we have for a coffee pot." Gunderson grinned. "Not complaining about the cooks, mind you, but it would seem *somebody* would be able to make consistent coffee in that thing."

"Hardly ever made by the same man twice," Johnson said. "And it depends on how much water they dip out of the water wagon, and how many o' those waxed paper packs of Arbuckle's is put into it."

"Sometimes it comes out a pale amber, and other times a deep brown," Ormond said.

"But it always tastes like hell," Gunderson finished. "What do *you* think of the food?" he asked St. Cyril.

"Since I'm an outsider, I take most of my meals in town," the reporter said. "But, I agree, that coffee *is* bad . . . unless it's flavored up with a dash of something stronger."

"Well, I rely on that coffee to keep me awake, most days," Ormond said. "If I put anything alcoholic in it, I'd be asleep within the hour."

"What's the latest rumor about the regiment moving out to Florida?" St. Cyril asked. "I've been here going on two weeks, and I've about wrung all the news I can get out of this camp."

"The way they've stepped up drill and are ragging us about details, I'd say they're putting on the finishing touches to make sure we're ready to go," Gunderson said.

"Would you say . . . another week?"

"Probably less."

"Hope you're right," Ormond said. "I'm getting mighty bored with drill, drill, and more drill."

"Can't wait to evict the chiggers, mosquitoes, and centipedes who've taken up residence with us in that tent," Gunderson said.

"It's hot, but leastways I got me a place to sleep inside on a cot in the exhibition hall," Johnson said with a grin.

Gunderson's estimate was right. Three days later, on May 28th, the Rough Riders were eating their noon meal, most sitting in the hot sun with only the shade of their hats, while others clustered in what scant shade they could find.

An orderly reported to the headquarters tent with some dispatches for Colonel Wood. Several minutes later, Lieutenant Colonel Theodore Roosevelt came out of the tent with a yellow telegram in hand. "Boys, we got our orders!"

He gave a whoop and threw his hat into the air. The Rough Riders erupted in a roar of appreciation. As the news of their impending departure spread, the rest of the day was given over to packing up and striking camp. The officers and non-coms had a hard time keeping the boisterous men at work after receiving the news.

"Finally off to Cuba!" Ormond said. Even though he couldn't yet think of himself as a Rough Rider, he was beginning to feel an *esprit de corps* with these men—a sense of belonging that, as a perpetual drifter and loner, he'd never experienced before. By the time the bugler blew "Taps" that night, he was thoroughly exhausted by all the excitement and work. Nothing left to do on the morrow but strike their tents and load the horses and gear onto the train cars waiting on the siding to take them to Tampa.

But this process proved to be much more complicated than he expected. Company by company the men rode out of their windy, dusty camp late Sunday afternoon, May 29th. What they found at the railroad siding was mass confusion.

"Should have known this wasn't going to be a smooth operation," Ormond groaned as the men were ordered to dismount, except for the leading troop that was to load first.

Colonel Roosevelt assumed personal charge of the operation when the frustrated trainmen appeared to be overwhelmed and ignorant of what was needed by the hundreds of mounted men. Through the drifting dust, Ormond could see the stocky commander waving his arms and pointing.

Several minutes stretched into an hour as the confusion was gradually sorted out. Under Roosevelt's direction, the officers of each troop, helped by ten hand-picked men, began to load. Company by company, the men unsaddled their horses and led them into the pens to water tanks and feed troughs. While the horses were occupied, the men lashed their saddles, bridles, and personal gear, tagged the bundles with their names and company letter. These were piled into a baggage car, along with as many sacks of grain and bales of hay as the car would hold. When the horses were fed and watered, they were driven up a chute into a stock car just behind a baggage car.

As they waited their turn, the men of Company C, keeping their horses within reach, lounged, chatted, sweated, and fretted. Dusk crept over the scene, and torches were lighted while the work went on. With sunset, the wind died, allowing the heat to wrap itself about them. The dust was still scuffed into clouds by the milling horses. Veils of fine particles drifted down, sticking to sweaty skin, reddening eyes, clogging nostrils, and forming grit between teeth and pipe stems.

A chuffing switch engine shuttled back and forth, banging couplings, repositioning, so the baggage car-stock car-baggage car arrangement was maintained.

"Now what?" Ormond asked a sergeant directing the loading. Their carbines and bedrolls were stowed, but there was no sign of passenger coaches for the men.

"Stand aside," the sergeant said, dismissing them with a wave of his hand. "Several more companies to load yet."

Iron shod hoofs clattered against boards as a half-broken horse balked at being funneled up the loading chute.

The operation dragged on in a somewhat orderly fashion until nearly midnight.

"Hell, they'll be at this until daylight," a man from Troop B growled. "Let's slide out of here and get a drink."

Five men from A and E Companies who'd drifted over

to chat joined him and they disappeared into the darkness.

"Where they gonna get a drink this time o' night?" Ormond asked Gunderson.

"There's at least four hole-in-the-wall bars around the stockyards."

"I could use a cold beer myself to cut this dust out of my throat."

"Like as not, you'd get knocked in the head and your watch stolen."

"I don't have a watch."

"They won't know that until after they knock you in the head."

Sometime later, Colonel Roosevelt approached Captain Alexander, standing nearby, supervising. Roosevelt's tailor-made tan uniform was streaked with dark sweat stains. He removed his hat and glasses. His round face was red in the flickering torchlight as he mopped it with his blue polka dot neckerchief. "Captain, men are straggling all over the place, mixing with other troops. And I know there are several who've gone off to those vile drinking establishments. Send a detail to search for them. Also, get the buglers to sound assembly until the first sergeants have them all rounded up and accounted for in their own troops."

"Yes, sir." Captain Alexander saluted and turned to obey.

More than an hour later, the loading was finished and the companies reassembled. Roosevelt could be heard berating the harried railroad crew. They received word that the passenger coaches had been delayed. Officers ordered the men to lie down where they were to get what sleep they could until morning.

"Wish I'd kept my blanket with me," Gunderson said as

they scraped around in the darkness, crushing down dead brush near the tracks to find a suitable bed.

"At the rate this outfit is moving, the Spanish will be long gone before we even get started for Florida."

"Or, they'll be so reinforced, we'll never get ashore in Cuba."

"More'n likely, the regular Army will rout 'em outta there in a few days."

"Never underestimate the enemy. That's what I did when we lost that herd of horses."

"I hope our new friend, Dismas Saint Cyril, isn't here to report on the lightning swiftness of the Rough Riders. He'd more'n likely send his paper the sketch of a turtle."

"This is the first time the regiment has moved together as a unit. Things will go a lot smoother next time. Just you wait." Gunderson wriggled into a more comfortable position, using his rolled-up jacket for a pillow.

Ormond yawned. The general stirring of several hundred men began to subside. "Don't let the bedbugs bite."

"Bedbugs are civilized. They live in bunkhouses and such places."

"Well, *something's* out here in the wild," Ormond said, scratching under his blue flannel shirt.

But, tired as he was, Ormond could have slept on a bed of nails. Next thing he knew he opened his eyes to the clear notes of "Reveille", punctuated by the banging of rail car couplings. The passenger coaches had arrived, broken into several small trains. Then began a general shuffling as the cars were mixed and matched to get all the men and baggage and horses of each company adjacent to each other in separate sections. Spreading out this way would give the officers of each troop time to unload, feed, and water the stock at each stopping place before the next troop arrived.

The trip to Florida took four long, dusty days. Many of the feed and watering stops took place at night, so men and officers were up all night, stumbling around in the half dark, then catching what sleep they could the following day in the jolting, upright seats. Two, double cane-backed seats were occupied by only three soldiers. They stacked their personal gear in the fourth seat.

Ormond and Gunderson lost track of Millard Johnson when the troops were separated. Ormond, staring out the coach window at the monotonous pine scrub, slowly passing water tanks and crossroad stores, found himself longing for the company of the older black man. The ex-slave always had some insights and ways of looking at things that were refreshingly candid.

At least one other person with a different perspective was also roaming the cars of this train, pencil and pad in hand—Dismas St. Cyril, the slightly cynical Chicago reporter. He seemed to appear when things were at their dullest, and, at that moment, he entered the car, swinging along the aisle, the satchel with his writing material and sketchbook slung from one shoulder.

"Ah, Peter Ormond, my friend," he said, shoving Ormond's drawn-up legs aside to make room for himself in the adjacent seat.

"Where you been?"

"Spent the last seven hours on the train just ahead with B Company." He sighed and reached for a slim cigar in his shirt pocket. His lean cheeks bore a fine, blond stubble as the reporter lit his smoke. His white shirt was grimy and wrinkled. "I thought this assignment would provide me with more than enough material. But, so far, it's been a most unenlivening trip. Richard Harding Davis is probably already in Tampa, getting all the news . . . or making some up."

"I tried reading one of his novels, but couldn't really get into it. Formula stuff."

"Nonetheless, he's the darling of the rich and famous. The New York *Herald* hired him to cover this. I can just picture him on some cool verandah, washing down his oysters with quarts of champagne and sharing jokes with the generals." The smoke from St. Cyril's cigar raveled away on a humid Alabama breeze. The sun-warped boards of an abandoned depot slid past the open window.

"Even the crowds that used to cheer us at every stop are gone," Ormond said.

"Yep. Just a few tired old souls here and there, waving," St. Cyril agreed. "The bloom is off the rose and you're still on American soil."

"Well . . . most of the older men in this part of the country wore Confederate gray only a generation ago. You can't expect a lot of wild enthusiasm for the Stars and Stripes."

"All Southerners aren't bitter," St. Cyril pointed out. "Look at those folks who've brought us watermelons and peaches and pails of milk."

"A lot of curious young girls who want to get a look at the boys in blue. But, I guess you're right. Can't generalize. And, speaking of food, I could sure do with a cup of coffee."

"Yep. The boys in B Company were complaining they haven't had any java since we left San Antone."

As if on cue, the door opened at the end of the car and Major Brodie came in. The popular officer stopped midway in the aisle. "Listen up, men. None of these way stations we've seen has the capacity to provide coffee for several hundred. So we've wired ahead to Waycross, Georgia, a big rail crossroads. They'll have plenty of coffee ready for every man when we get there sometime tonight."

A spontaneous cheer greeted this announcement. Spirits picked up immediately. The rest of the day was filled with anticipation. Ormond could almost smell roasted coffee beans at every siding.

The train finally pulled into Waycross just after dark, to be greeted by committees of ladies bearing sandwiches, cake, and lemonade. Gunderson and Ormond joined the streams of men piling off the cars, and followed their noses into the waiting room marked **Whites Only**. Huge restaurant-type urns were steaming with fresh coffee. The crowd was six deep at the urns as the attendants served up the coffee in heavy mugs—a nickel per cup. More soldiers jammed into the room. Coffee went to a dime. The doorways were blocked with more men struggling to get inside. Coffee rose to a quarter a cup. The depot waiting room was a milling mass of Rough Riders.

"A quarter for coffee!" came the cry from those in front. *"A quarter for coffee!"* The angry shout was passed back through the crowd.

Two men and two women behind the counter were getting flustered and began to swear at those who were grabbing filled mugs and refusing to pay. Then the servers began to look panicked as a growl rose from the mob. Righteous anger swelled. A sudden crash of glass or wood could trigger a riot. The pent-up frustration of hundreds of Rough Riders would have wrecked the place.

"A quarter a cup!" The words rolled like the foghorn of doom back through the cars on the siding.

Ormond and Gunderson had not yet reached the counter and were pinned in the crush of bodies. Ormond knew a moment of panic, fearing a potential riot.

"Make way!" Major Brodie came clawing his way through the mass, shoving men aside. "Stop selling that coffee!" he shouted. He fought his way to the counter. Red-faced, he confronted the man in charge. "You're selling these men coffee the government has already paid for. Sell another cup and I'll put you under arrest, damn you!" he shouted. Then he turned to the crowd. "Get on back to your trains!" he ordered. "You'll get coffee . . . every one of you. They sold you your own coffee, so they'll have to make it good. You'll get it."

The waiting room was cleared and guards put on the doors.

"I wouldn't be in that man's shoes for any amount of money," Ormond said, glancing back at the vendor who was standing mute in the face of Major Brodie's tirade.

Shortly after, four men appeared in the aisle of the coach carrying the Buzzacot oven wash boiler full of coffee. The men dipped their pint cups in it as it passed. Before they pulled out of the station, heading south, every man's belly was sloshing with as much of the tasty brew as he could hold.

"I must be getting awfully tired," Ormond said, rubbing his eyes.

"We all are."

"No, I mean to the point of having hallucinations. I could've sworn I saw somebody I recognized back there on that depot platform."

"Anybody I know?"

"The woman on the train I told you about who stole my old man's gold coins."

Gunderson gave him a sideways look. "If so, she really gets around."

"I know it's not likely. Just some black-haired woman who resembled her."

"Try to get some sleep and forget about it. Those coins are preying on your mind."

"Yeah."

They were out of supplies. The quartermaster had been assured the trip would take only three days and had provisioned the trains accordingly. The journey was now into its fourth day, and hand-outs from well-wishers didn't go far enough to satisfy the hunger of several hundred soldiers. At every stop, volunteers, often with the encouragement of their officers, slipped off the train in search of unattended pigs, chickens, or geese. When the train started rolling again, the stolen pigs and fowl were butchered and cooked over wood stoves in the ends of the cars.

At Gainesville, Florida, foragers from Captain McClintock's troop snatched several small pigs found rooting in feeding pens next to the tracks. The station agent, who owned the animals, happened to see the theft and complained to Major Brodie. The major came into the car, mustache bristling. "Release those pigs immediately!" he roared. "Do you want the Rough Riders to get the reputation as common thieves? We need the support of the people . . . not their hatred."

The men scrambled, shame-faced, to toss the pigs off or let them down out of the windows on the depot side. But the piglets ran back under the cars toward their pens and were scooped up by waiting troopers who hid them in the next car.

As the steam whistle gave a short blast and the train jerked forward, the station agent strutted up and down the platform, spouting to his friends: "Those sons-of-bitches ain't going to get away with no hogs of mine!"

Chapter Seven

"Form for attack! Forward!"

A single note from the bugler started the line abreast, carbines at the ready. Ormond and Gunderson surged ahead at a fast walk through the palmetto scrub. A minute later, a more distant bugle sounded the order to move Company D up to support.

"Company C . . . the line, double time!"

Shouted commands were relayed from the mounted major to captains to lieutenants to sergeants to troops. The ragged line of men broke into a run and flopped down at a designated mark, heedless of rattlers, tarantulas, or scorpions.

"Commence firing! Fire at will!"

Instead of the concentrated roar of gunfire, the line erupted with the clicking of hundreds of empty rifles and the ratcheting of bolts being cocked.

"I can't wait till we get to mounted drill," Gunderson grunted. Sweat dripped off his nose as he snapped his Krag at an imaginary enemy.

"Tomorrow will be the second day we've been here," Ormond replied. "The horses ought to be rested from the trip by then."

Gunderson pushed up his gray campaign hat and wiped a sleeve across his face. "Cuba couldn't be hotter than this. M'gun barrel feels like it's been fired."

"The water's pouring off me. I'll trade the dry Arizona desert for this any day." Ormond took a deep breath. "One of the boys was saying rattlers and coral snakes live in this palmetto scrub."

"Don't think about it," Gunderson said. "We've made enough noise to scare off a legion of snakes."

"Well, I plan to make even more."

"Company C . . . forward!"

The line of riflemen sprang up and rushed ahead, Ormond yelling and tromping noisily.

"Lie down. Commence firing!"

Ormond and Gunderson fanned the grass before them with their carbines and flopped down in the space that was hopefully cleared of venomous snakes. The staccato clicking rippled up and down the line.

"Why the hell didn't they use tactics like this during the Civil War?" Ormond panted, working his bolt, "instead of charging breastworks while standing up in ranks?"

"Ever try to muzzle-load a long musket while you're belly down?" Gunderson asked. "Breechloaders make this prone position possible. War is a lot more comfortable these days."

"Company C . . . forward!" the sergeant shouted.

The process was repeated and they flopped down forty yards farther along.

"*Yeeoow!*" Ormond sprang up, slapping wildly at his forearm. "Snake!"

Gunderson raked the coarse grass aside with his weapon. "A scorpion nailed you. Nothing to fear."

"The hell you say! It burns like a hornet sting!" Ormond

gasped, pulling back his sleeve and rubbing the spot on his forearm where he'd landed on the insect.

"You . . . get down!" the sergeant yelled.

Ormond dropped.

"Glad it was a scorpion," Gunderson said with a straight face. "Otherwise you might have swole up from the poison and died, 'cause there ain't a drop of snakebite remedy around here . . . this being a dry county."

"I've had about enough of this damned foolishness," Ormond said, retrieving his carbine.

Gunderson glanced at the sun. "It's almost noon. The officers will have us knock off shortly."

Next day the Rough Riders conducted mounted drill. It was a decided improvement, even for a novice horseman like Peter Ormond. After dismissal, several of the men, led by Gunderson, pulled off the saddles and galloped their mounts bareback on the nearby beach and through the surf. The horses seemed to enjoy the cool spray as much as the men.

"*Whew!* What a relief!" Ormond said, sliding off to stand knee deep in the low-breaking waves.

Gunderson joined him. "Better wet with sea water than with sweat, I always say."

"Yeah. That was always your practice in southern Arizona, was it?" Ormond laughed, wiping water from his eyes.

After twenty minutes, Ormond said: "Let's get back and hit the mess line."

A half hour later they were shuffling past the long table, having their mess tins filled. Some distance beyond, in the scant shade of three tall palms, two men toiled at the Buzzacot oven. One was Millard Johnson, wearing a straw hat. But they were too far away to get his attention.

The two men found a bare spot on the ground and sat

cross-legged to eat. "Johnson makes a great stew," Gunderson said, spooning up the meat and potatoes.

"Yeah. Wish we could figure out a way to eat this, too." Ormond pointed at a square of hardtack. "I saw one of the fifty-pound boxes this stuff is packed in. Stenciled on the lid was . . . 'Army Bread from the Union Mechanical Baking Company, Baltimore, Maryland.' I have a feeling it's left over from the last war."

Gunderson picked up his piece of hardtack. "What are these pin holes for? To let in air so they'll be nice and fluffy?" He rapped it on the edge of his metal plate.

"Weevils. No extra charge."

"Let's try this," Gunderson said, placing the hunk of hardtack in his mess kit lid. Drawing his Colt, he used the butt as a hammer to crush the biscuit, then dumped the resulting small chunks and crumbs into his stew.

"Good idea." Ormond followed his example. "I've been soaking it in coffee. That works, too."

After lunch, the soldiers were free for the day. Some dozed away the hottest hours in their tents. Others broke out well-worn decks of cards. Gambling was discouraged, but the officers looked the other way as the men whiled away their free hours with poker or craps.

The teamsters had another type of contest. They paired off, one on one, and cracked their long blacksnake whips at one another's legs. When a leaping teamster failed to avoid the end of this opponent's lash, it raised a welt, even through a leather boot. More importantly, he lost a point in the competition.

That afternoon, Gunderson decided to take a nap, while Ormond wandered off to the edge of camp, looking for a breeze. What he found was Dismas St. Cyril, seated on a stump in the shade, sketch pad on his knees.

Ormond paused to watch the artist at work.

"Thought my editor might be interested in this." St. Cyril jabbed his pencil toward a line of soldiers waiting outside the chaplain's tent. "Gives a different perspective on the glories of war."

"What's that?"

"Paroxysms of piety. Baptisms, confessions, or conferences . . . not sure." Holding the pencil sideways, he shaded in a spot on the pad. "Why do men suddenly become religious when they find out they're going into battle?"

"Fear of being killed and going to hell, of course."

"Exactly." He chuckled. "You sound as cynical as I usually do." St. Cyril studied the single line of lounging, chatting men from various units. Some were Rough Riders. "I'll bet, if you took a poll, at least half the men in that line haven't seen the inside of a church in the past three months."

"You're saying they only turn to God when they're scared."

"Human nature."

"Actually Chaplain Brown's open air services have been pretty well attended since we got here." Ormond knelt on one knee and leaned his elbows on the other. "I take it you're not a believer."

"Not in the conventional way," St. Cyril replied, keeping his eyes on his sketch pad. "I believe in a Supreme Being. A man would be a fool to look at the complexities of the natural world and not see there is some master intelligence behind it all."

"But you don't believe in a personal God?"

"I think the Almighty, or whatever name He goes by, started the earth and planets to spinning and walked off to take care of some other business. We're pretty much on our own to fight it out with each other and the animals for survival." He smiled thinly. "I don't claim any special insight. Some of our founding fathers had much the same idea. Called themselves Deists."

"What about an afterlife?"

St. Cyril made a few deft strokes and the figure of a man emerged on his pad. "I've given that considerable thought over the years. I'm what's known in the trade as an agnostic . . . don't know, and have no means of finding out. If we live after we die, so be it. If we don't. . . ." He shrugged. "But I'm not going to waste my time thinking about it. I'm a practicing hedonist."

Ormond fell silent for several minutes, fascinated by the skill of the artist as he brought to life the line of men waiting patiently at the chaplain's tent.

"You speak like a well-educated man," Ormond finally said.

"Dropped out of college when I ran out of money. Parents couldn't help 'cause they were barely on the high side of poverty. Grandpa Saint Cyril was a wealthy newspaper owner in France, but he lost everything except his life when he fled the bloody aftermath of the revolution. English friends smuggled him out in an ox cart just ahead of a horde of the red-capped brotherhood who wanted to guillotine him. Probably just as well that the family fell on hard times. If I had money, I probably would have died of excess, instead of having to work for a living." He paused to make several careful lines, then went back to the broad, sweeping strokes. "Grandpa Saint Cyril was a staunch Catholic, but quit the church after he finally arrived in America."

"Why?"

"Disillusioned. He lost faith in the perfectibility of man. After the brutality of the so-called reformers who overthrew the monarchy, he couldn't continue to believe that humans contained any spark of divinity or grace. He used to say that humans were only a higher form of animal, acting on emotion and instinct, instead of reason and free will."

"Maybe it looks that way *en masse,* but Christianity teaches that salvation is a matter of individual choice and action."

"It would be nice to think so." The artist sighed. "But, for better or worse, only my late mother was a practicing believer in much of anything since Grandfather's day. She was a British Anglican. She's the one who named me Dismas, after the so-called good thief who was crucified alongside Christ. And my surname, Saint Cyril, is taken directly from an early saint. You'd think, with two names like that, there might have been hope for me." He laughed as he swept off his broad-brimmed hat and wiped a sleeve across his brow. "Besides, righteous people are so deadly serious, don't you think? To my knowledge, there's not a single reference in the Bible to Christ ever laughing or sharing a joke with his Apostles. Surely, laughter is one of the great things in life."

"Laughter's the result of the ridiculous, or ludicrous, or of irony, is it not?" Ormond was on shaky ground here. "Christ didn't deal in any of those things. He was God."

"Ah, but He was human, also."

"You're right. I just don't know." Ormond was no apologist and regretted getting into this discussion. "I'm thirsty." He stood up and stretched. "Gunderson and I are pulling guard duty tonight, so we'll have passes to town tomorrow. Maybe we'll see you there."

"Maybe. I'm going to Fifth Corps headquarters at the Plant Hotel in Tampa in the morning. General Shafter is there with his staff. Maybe I can pick up some news."

"Why Washington would appoint a general who weighs over three hundred pounds to command this expedition in the field is beyond me."

"He's got a good military record," St. Cyril said. "That's all I know."

The next afternoon Gunderson and Ormond took advantage of their passes to clean up and go to town. Passes were not at premium since there was little to do there. But it broke the routine. The end of the trolley line into Tampa was just over a mile walk from their camp. A few messmates accompanied them, but went their own way when they reached town. The two men wandered up and down the hard-packed, sandy streets, poking through the small shops and getting a curt reception from the storekeepers. Some were outright rude, ordering them to leave if they weren't going to buy something.

"Natives not nearly so friendly as those we met on the way down here," Ormond commented.

Gunderson nodded. "Several thousand soldiers been here a few weeks now. I hear tell they've made themselves pretty much of a nuisance . . . drunken brawls, thefts, rapes, even a couple of stabbings at local whorehouses."

"With these tan britches and leggings we don't look anything like the blue of the regular Army or the other volunteer units."

"Makes no difference to the locals. We're all just hell-raisin' soldiers, black and white, in whatever uniform. Captain said decent women have taken to staying indoors after dark and everyone locks the doors. They like our money, but can't wait for us to leave."

"Speaking of money, when do we get paid?"

"I think the paymaster is due to set up his tent tomorrow. We're about a month's pay behind. And it ain't gonna be near what I was fixin' to get for those horses we lost." He shook his head at the thought. "Life sure takes some funny twists and turns."

A familiar voice hailed them: "Well, two of the boys from Company C!" Dismas St. Cyril came striding up and dropped the stub of his cigar in the sand, grinding it out. "A little early in the day for a spree, isn't it?"

"How does a man go on a spree in a dry town?" Gunderson asked.

"Too bad you couldn't pass for newsmen. I've just come from Fifth Corps headquarters at the Plant Hotel. Free food and drink for military brass and all of us lowly toilers of the pen. Richard Harding Davis was there, of course, as was Ed Marshall. One writes great things about the Rough Riders, and the other can't say anything good about Roosevelt and the First Volunteer Cavalry. Ed has nothing against the rank and file, but he hates Roosevelt. Called him an arrogant warmonger and a glory hound to boot. Nice fella, that Marshall." He grinned. "Speaks his mind."

Ormond caught a whiff of alcohol on the reporter's breath.

"If this heat has made you thirsty, I might be able to fix you up with a highball," St. Cyril said.

"Thought that was a railroad term," Gunderson said.

"A high-class Eastern drink made with rye or bourbon."

"I wouldn't mind a shot," Gunderson said.

"I'm not into the hard stuff," Ormond said, "but I could sure use a cold beer."

"Can't help you with that," St. Cyril said. "But I know an ice cream parlor you might fancy."

"Well, if I can't get a beer, an ice cream soda might hit the spot," Ormond said.

"This is a very special ice cream parlor," St. Cyril said with a wink over his shoulder as he led the way.

In the middle of the next block, the reporter went up onto a porch. The two windows were bordered with white lace curtains. Inside, a few local couples were eating ice cream. Behind the counter were rows of home-freezing ice cream cylinders. Cardboard signs on the walls advertised **Try our General Robert E. Lee Milk Shake, General Miles Grape Juice, A General Beauregard Favorite—Mint Ice Cream**. Equal space for both Northern and Southern generals. The owner of this place was catering to everyone.

Behind the counter was a sign in smaller letters, stating: **No Alcoholic Liquor Sold Here**.

"A rye highball," St. Cyril said softly.

"Sorry, gentlemen. Nothing like that sold here."

"We're soldiers in the Rough Riders," Gunderson explained.

"A highball," St. Cyril repeated. "Rye or bourbon."

"What's that drink? High . . . something? That's liquor, ain't it? No liquor here." He pointed at the sign behind him. "I'm mighty sorry, boys, but you've been misinformed. This is a dry county. Maybe you'd like some ice cream? That General Grant Ice Cream Soda's mighty tasty."

Ormond and Gunderson looked at each other, then at St. Cyril. The reporter seemed perplexed.

"Maybe you boys would like to set and rest a spell before you go traipsin' out looking for what this town can't supply, nohow. You boys go on out back and take a chair under the arbor. It's mighty restful there and I know you boys are tired."

Apparently St. Cyril had been mistaken. The trio retired

out the back door to the shady arbor.

"I wouldn't be disappointed, but I had my mouth all fixed for a whiskey," Gunderson said.

Ormond hadn't expected to find a beer, so he had been eyeing the ice cream menu.

"Damn, Saint Cyril, that was a mighty shabby joke," Gunderson said as the three sat down in rocking chairs. The sun made a dappled pattern on the ground as a breeze rustled the overhead leaves. It was a very peaceful setting, and St. Cyril didn't reply to the complaint. White clouds mushroomed in the distance, heralding the usual afternoon rain shower that was probably two hours away.

"How you gentlemen enjoying yourselves?" the proprietor's voice came from inside the store. Right behind the voice came the man himself, wearing his white apron and carrying a tray with three tall glasses beaded with moisture. Ice tinkled as he handed each of them a glass. "I'm hopin' these will be something you gentlemen won't mind partaking of. It's a temperance drink, you know. We don't sell nothing but temperance drinks. Law's against it."

Whatever it was, it tasted marvelous. Ormond was not familiar with hard mixed drinks, but this cold concoction had a fruity flavor, slid down smoothly, and had a slight bite to it.

"You boys had me puzzled when you said highball. Never heard of it. That a New York drink? This here is a . . . well, you might say a General Grant Ice Cream Soda, if anybody should ask you. Or you could call it a General Miles Milk Shake. Anyway, it's a military drink, if you get what I mean." He chuckled. "Anybody in uniform or a member of the press can get any drink he wants. This here is bourbon."

"Mighty kind of you," Gunderson said, savoring another sip.

The proprietor grinned and left with the tray under his arm.

The men rocked and sipped for a minute or two, enjoying the breeze and the drinks.

"To make this afternoon complete, I've got something here you might like to read," St. Cyril said, pulling a section of folded newspaper from his hip pocket.

"Something you wrote?"

"I wish I had. No, it's the latest Mister Dooley column by Finley Peter Dunne in the Chicago *Evening Post*."

"Ah, one of my favorite columnists!" Ormond exclaimed, reaching for the paper. "But where I was living, I couldn't get a Chicago paper very often."

Gunderson looked curious.

"If you're not familiar with Mister Dooley, let me read some of this to you. It's written in an Irish dialect, but I'll translate as I go. Martin J. Dooley is a fictitious Chicago bartender, a middle-aged bachelor, who holds forth on all kinds of topics when his friend and customer, Hennessy, comes in." He held the paper in one hand. "This is titled 'Mules and Others'.

" 'I see,' said Mister Dooley, 'the first great land battle of the war has been fought.'

" 'Where was that?' demanded Mister Hennessy in great excitement. 'Lord save us, but where was that?'

" 'The Alger guards,' said Mister Dooley, 'broke from the corral where they had them tied up, eatin' thistles, and made a desperate charge on the camp at Tampa. They descended like a whirlwind, driving the astonished troops before them, and then charged back again, completin' their errand of destruction. At the last account the brave soldiers

116

was climbin' trees and telegraph poles, and the regiment of mules was kickin' the pink silk linin' out of the officers' quarters. The gallant mules was led by a most courageous jackass, and 'tis understood that me friend, Mack, will appoint him a brigadier-general just as soon as he can find out who his father is. 'Tis too bad he'll have no children to perpetuate the fame of him. He went through the camp at the head of his troops of mules without castin' a shoe. He's the biggest jackass in Tampa today, not exceptin' the censor, and I doubt if there's a bigger one in Washington, though I could name a few that could try a race with him. Anyhow, they'll know how to reward him. They know a jackass when they see one, and they see a good many in that peaceful city.

" 'The charge of Tampa'll go into history as the first land action of the war. And by the way, Hennessy, if this here sociable is to go on at the present rate, I'm strong on armin' the wild Army mules and the unbridled jackasses of the prairie and give them a chance to set Cuba free.' "

Ormond paused in his reading as a guffaw split the sunburned face of Gunderson. St. Cyril merely smiled and sipped at his drink.

Ormond read on down the column, pausing often to chuckle. "And here's the last of it . . . 'Ye don't see the difference, says ye. They ain't any of the leaders. As efficient a lot of mules as ever exposed their ears. The trouble is with the rank and file. They're men. What's needed to carry on this war as it goes today is an army of jacks and mules. When ye say to a man . . . "Git up, whoa, gee, back up, get along!" . . . he don't know what you're drivin' at, or to. But a mule hears the orders with a melancholy smile, droops his ears, and follows his warm, moist breath. The orders from Washington is perfectly comprehensible to a jackass, but they don't mean anythin' to a poor, foolish man. No human being, Hennessy, can understand what the devil use it was to sink a ship that cost two hundred thousand dollars and was worth at least eighty dollars in Santiago Harbor, if we have to keep fourteen ships outside to prevent five Spanish ships from sailin'. The poor, tired human mind don't tumble, Hennessy, to the reason for landin' four hundred marines at Guantanamo to clear the forest, when Havana is livin' free on hot tamales and ice cream. . . .

" 'We need what Hogan calls the *esprit de corpse* and we'll only have it when the mules begin to move.'

" 'I should think,' said Mister Hennessy, 'now that the jackasses has begun to be uneasy. . . .'

" 'We ought to be afraid the Cabinet and the Board of Strategy'll be stampeded?' Mister Dooley interrupted. 'Never fear. They're too near the fodder.' "

For the next two hours the men sat in the shade of the arbor, sipping, ordering another, and sipping them as the sun slid toward the Gulf. Feeling rather mellow, they adjourned to the steps of the front porch with the owner and finished off with dishes of ice cream. They watched the mounted Provost Guards of the Negro 10th Cavalry rounding up men who had no passes or overstayed their leave, and herding them back to camp.

"Mighty sad sight," the proprietor remarked as three soldiers trudged along dejectedly in front of the mounted guard.

Nobody spoke for several seconds as the parade passed.

"It don't seem right for a nigra on horseback to be roundin' up white folk," the owner continued. "It gravels us folks around here to see that," he said. "I figure it's the Army way and all proper and legal, but it's almost like they're rubbing our noses in it, you know?"

"It's the uniform, not the man," Ormond tried to explain.

"I know, but it don't seem natural, somehow. Ever punch one of those black bastards?"

"Black bastards, white bastards . . . it's all the same. Punch a Provost Guard and we're in deep trouble," Gunderson said. "The Army has strict discipline."

"But not much tact or sense," Ormond finished under his breath.

"I'd be obliged if you boys would have another General Grant Ice Cream Soda . . . on me."

"Thanks, but our passes run out at six," Ormond said, standing up. "We'd best be gettin' back."

They shook hands with the kindly store owner and departed toward camp, St. Cyril walking rather unsteadily behind.

Chapter Eight

Three days later, they received orders to embark for Cuba. The excitement was tinged with frustration when the men also learned that several companies would be left behind in Tampa. It appeared there were not enough transport ships to haul them all. To make matters worse, the Rough Riders were forbidden to bring their horses. The only animals allowed were the officers' personal mounts, along with horses and mules to pull the caissons and mountain howitzers, and to serve as pack animals.

Ormond digested this news, secretly glad he would not have to test his limited riding skills on a half-wild mustang while under fire in some jungle.

Gunderson slammed his campaign hat in the dirt. "I spent most of my working life on a horse," he grumbled. "All that mounted drill we've been through . . . for nothing! Was that Colonel Wood's order?"

"It probably came down from above him. So they could save room on the ships for men and supplies . . . not horses."

Gunderson shook his head. "Instead of Roosevelt's

Rough Riders, Saint Cyril and the press will be calling us Wood's Weary Walkers."

"Better afoot than not at all."

The two men joined others crowding around the trunk of a tall palm near their tent row. An orderly was tacking up a notice.

There were gripes and curses as the closest read the list of those to be left behind. "What's it say?" men in back were calling. "What about Company H?"

"Quit your shovin'! You'll get a turn."

Ormond and Gunderson elbowed their way to the front. A quick glance turned Ormond's stomach to jelly. Captain Alexander's Company C was to be left behind, along with Companies H, I, and M of the Rough Riders. Other volunteer units and some of the regular infantry and cavalry units were listed as well, but Ormond hardly noticed them. His eyes had stopped on their own Company C. "This can't be." He swallowed back the lump in his throat. The depth of disappointment made him realize how much he'd counted on going to Cuba with his comrades-in-arms.

"This ain't the end of it." Grim-faced, Gunderson guided him out of the throng. "The size of the companies are being cut to seventy men each," he continued. "If we want to get there, we'd best get t'hustlin'."

"What?" Ormond was still in shock.

"We ain't come all this way just to be told we're gonna sit around this hole. There'll be a lot of swappin' and dealin' going on. So we need to figure a way to buy us a couple o' slots in a company that's scheduled to go."

"How? We aren't personal friends of Roosevelt or Colonel Wood, or even Major Brodie, so it's not like we can swing any influence."

"Some of Roosevelt's college friends might use influence. We gotta use money. Money. That's the key. Some of these men can be bought. They'll give up their places if we can make it worth their while." He looked at the crowd around the posted notice. A few men were having lively discussions. Several were jogging toward the next row of white tents that housed Captain O'Neill's A Troop. "We'd better get a move on. The trading has started."

"I cashed and spent my last post office pay check on the way down here. I have the thirteen-fifty I was paid the other day . . . less than a month's wages for a private. That's not going to induce anyone to stay behind."

"I'm about busted, too. Poker took nearly all I got for my Winchester and Colt. As I see it, we have only one chance."

"What's that?"

"Use one of those gold coins Millard Johnson has."

"Oh, no."

Gunderson shrugged. "The only other thing we have of value between us is that nickel-plated, ivory-gripped Bisley Colt you're totin'. And I don't think that's worth enough to buy us both a place."

"How much do you think it will take?"

"I'm guessin' fifty dollars. Five hundred, tops, if the bidding gets fierce. One of those Eastern dudes might be able to part with that much."

Ormond struggled with this for several seconds. "I hate to give up my gun. On the other hand, even if I could persuade Johnson to part with one of those coins, it'd be worth at least a couple of thousand . . .'way more than we need."

"Well, it's your choice, 'cause they're your coins."

"No, they're my father's. But I've already lost most of them to a thief. Guess we might as well get something for one of those that's left. Let's go find Millard."

122

They located Johnson laying out food to prepare the noon meal. They motioned to him and he left the other cook tending the Buzzacot oven.

"You look kinda lean," Ormond said in greeting. Since arriving in Tampa, they'd seen him only from a distance. Johnson wore a sleeveless white cotton shirt. In place of the old straw hat, he'd fashioned himself something resembling a chef's hat from a cleverly folded newspaper.

"Smellin' food all day in this heat killed my appetite," he replied. "I'm hard muscle now." He grinned, flashing his white teeth. "Lost m'baby fat."

Ormond told him the situation. He half expected an argument, but Johnson merely pulled up his shirt and slid the belt around. He glanced about to be sure no one was watching, then used the tip of his big butcher knife to sever a few of the rough stitches that held the two layers together. "Which one you want?"

"Any of them will do. As far as their collector's value, I don't know one from another."

Johnson slipped his thumb and forefinger into the damp, sweaty leather and fished out a coin. It glowed softly in the sunlight as he handed it over.

Ormond looked closely at it. It was an 1849 $10 gold coin struck by the Oregon Exchange Company, depicting a beaver on the obverse side. "I hope whoever we pay with this realizes it's worth more than ten dollars."

"Since it's stolen, they'll maybe find out the hard way when they go to selling it," Johnson said.

"Not much chance anybody will know where it came from," Gunderson said.

"Knowing my old man, he's spread the word among coin dealers, banks, and big-time collectors around the country to be on the look-out for these."

Johnson pulled a large bandanna from his hip pocket and wiped a sheen of sweat from his face. "This gold don't appear as dear as it did a while back."

"I know. We've moved on to more important things," Ormond agreed. Time and distance had softened the arrogance of his aging father. The theft itself seemed to be fading into history. "Someday I'll force the old man to be proud of me, whether he'll admit it or not," he vowed. "But it won't be today. C'mon, let's go buy ourselves two tickets to Cuba."

"That's really a load off my mind," Gunderson said, swinging a wooden case of canned meat down to Ormond who grabbed it and shoved it onto the tailgate of a wagon.

"We had to take their work detail, too, but I don't mind a bit," Ormond said.

The next afternoon a dozen men were jacking food and supplies from boxcars on a siding and loading them onto wagons for transport to the ships.

"Hope we're long gone to Cuba before they find out that coin is hot," Ormond said, pausing to uncork his canteen for a long drink.

"Small chance they'll ever find out."

The two men were now officially members of Captain James McClintock's B Troop, having purchased their places from Sol Drachman, a clerk from Tucson, and Edward Collier, a teamster from Globe. These considerably wealthier Rough Riders would remain in Tampa with C Company.

Gunderson jerked another case off the stack and slid it toward the open doorway.

Ormond reached for it. "Look at this."

"What? U.S. Army?"

"Over on this side." Ormond pointed. "The original consignee."

The words **Yokohama, Japan** were burned into the wood.

"This stuff was canned for Jap soldiers in the China-Japan war of four years ago. It's marked roast beef." Ormond climbed onto the tailgate and stepped across into the freight car. "Think I'll have a look at what kind of leftovers we have from the Japs." He picked up a crowbar lying in the corner and levered the lid off one of the crates. Using his sheath knife, he punched a large hole in one of the cans. He stirred the brown, glutinous mixture with the knife blade and held the can to his nose. *"Whew!"* He poured the contents out onto the wooden floor and spread it around. "Ground up cow . . . bone, gristle, cartilage, and gullet with stringy fibers."

"Enough to make a man become a vegetarian," Gunderson said.

"Damn' Chicago packing houses, selling this to the Army!"

"Wouldn't you love to see Mister Armor, Mister Cudahy, and all the company directors dragged by their noses through a vat of this goop?" Gunderson scraped the mess toward the open door with the edge of his shoe.

It was late afternoon by the time they finished their freight detail and returned to camp.

"We missed lunch, and now we're too late for supper," Ormond groused. "I'm starved."

The Buzzacot oven had been dismantled and stacked for transport, except for two large pans with the remains of the noon meal. Johnson was nowhere in sight—only two soldiers on clean-up detail.

"Got anything left to eat?" Gunderson asked.

"Nope. Supper's over. Even the guards have been fed. Nothing left but what's in that pan we're fixin' to wash. And some cold coffee in that pot."

"We'll take it." Ormond snatched two clean tin plates and two cups. They scraped the leavings of the breaded meat and potato dish out of the corners of the big pan, poured themselves some tepid coffee, and sat down with their backs to a palm tree to eat.

Several minutes later, Ormond set his dish aside with a sigh. "When you're really hungry, anything tastes good."

"Yeah. Those leftovers been settin' out a few hours. The sun kept 'em warm."

"Waste not, want not."

"An army marches on its stomach."

Dusk was gathering when they finally reported to Company B. Most of their new comrades were only faces they'd seen in drill and formations, but it didn't matter. They'd get acquainted aboard ship.

"Hurry up, you two. Strike your dog tent," the sergeant ordered.

Everyone else was nearly packed to leave. The two men dropped their tent and unbuttoned it down the middle, each taking a half. Since the Rough Riders had to function as dismounted cavalry, the experienced sergeant was showing several of the men how to fashion a horse-collar roll to carry their belongings.

"OK, lay out your blanket . . . so," the sergeant said, demonstrating. "Then put the tent pegs and half of the two tent poles on it. Arrange your towel, socks, shirt and extra underwear, and roll up the blanket. Now, take your half of the tent and fold it lengthwise. This you lay on top of the blanket roll. Then tie it at the ends and in the middle."

The result looked like a reefed sail.

"Now, bend it until it has a horse-collar shape and fasten the two ends together. There you are . . . ready to stick your head through and sling it. One thing you must be careful of," the non-com cautioned. "The roll must be made sloppy . . . not neat. A hard horse collar will bear down on your shoulder like a steel bar. So roll it loose and sloppy for the part that lies across your shoulder, with your baggage fore and aft. You'll look like a bunch of hobos . . . blanket stiffs, if you will. But it works."

Ormond and Gunderson followed this advice, and, by the time it was full dark, they were standing in formation with their company, ready to march to the Tampa waterfront. There was some delay as they awaited orders to move.

Suddenly, as if on signal, Ormond was struck by a sharp pain in his stomach, a searing agony that doubled him over. "Oh!" The sword thrust of pain folded him over to the ground. And it was a long way to the latrine. His knees came up and his body broke out into a cold sweat. Gunderson had also been stricken and was writhing on the ground next to him. "Colic!" he gasped. "Or something worse."

Something violent was erupting inside them. There was no pretending that everything was all right.

"Sergeant, stay here and see to those men," Lieutenant Wilcox ordered.

Seconds later, a bugle sounded. The company swung into fours-right and marched away into the darkness toward Tampa.

So severe were the stabbing pains, Ormond was hardly aware of his surroundings. Waves of nausea engulfed him.

"Both of you are going to the regimental hospital."

With a supreme effort, they crawled and staggered like

127

two cripples to the spot where the hospital tent had stood. A hospital sergeant looked them over while the last of the medical supplies were being lashed down on the wagon. "Medicine's all packed up. You boys will have to go to the Army general hospital in Tampa."

"Where's Captain Stafford, our battalion surgeon?"

"In Tampa."

"We were well until a half hour ago. Put us on the wagon. We'll be all right in the morning."

"Can't be done. It's the general hospital for you."

The thought of missing the ship was nearly as bad as the grippe that had snared them in its vise.

The hospital sergeant went back to packing supplies. The two sick men stayed bent over by the wagon. The driver walked behind them. "Go down the road a piece, and I'll let you on," he whispered to them. "I'll be looking for you."

Ormond knew he couldn't get down the road or climb on anything. He couldn't even crawl up a ramp. He drew his knees up to his chin like a jackknife. Gunderson looked no better.

"Why the hell isn't this medical wagon loaded and gone?" a voice boomed out of the darkness. A horseman rode up. It was Major Brodie.

"Major," Ormond cried weakly. "We're just a little sick, but we've got to get to Cuba."

"They're really sick," the sergeant said. "They want to get on the medical wagon, but it's against orders. They need to be in the hospital."

"The hell they do. We need men in Cuba," Major Brodie said briskly. "What's wrong with them?"

"Just a stomach ache, major," Ormond answered quickly.

It was a stomach ache to end all stomach aches. It was poison witches' brew; it was hot pitchforks from hell.

"Can you ride the baggage wagon?" the major asked.

"Yes, sir." Ormond neglected to add that they couldn't climb up.

"Put 'em on," Major Brodie said. Then he was off into the darkness.

It took the driver and both sergeants to hoist the two men. They lay on the folded tents behind the driver. The wagon jerked into motion and bumped away toward Tampa. Ormond thought the pain could get no worse, but it did. "Sorry," he gasped through clenched teeth. "It's no fun having a couple of groaning invalids riding behind you."

"Don't mind me," the driver said. "Holler if you want. I know whatever you got must hurt." He clucked to the mules and slapped the reins over their backs.

"How . . . far . . . is it?" Ormond moaned, holding his breath against the pain as the wagon jolted over uneven ground.

"Not . . . as far . . . as it seems," Gunderson gasped.

Twice they asked the driver to stop so one and then the other could roll off the wagon, drop his pants, and surrender to the cramping of dysentery. Squatting in the darkness, Ormond felt as if he were losing part of his insides.

Shortly after midnight, they reached Tampa.

"There's a drugstore," Gunderson whispered. "We need morphine for the pain."

"It's closed."

"Can you stop a minute and strike a light for me?"

The driver pulled up. He raked a match across the wooden seat and lit a lantern hanging on the corner of the bed. Gunderson already had a pencil and paper out of his pocket and began scribbling.

"What're you doing?"

"I'm now Doctor Adolphus Smith, Army Medical Corps, and I just wrote a prescription for morphine."

"How do you know all the Latin abbreviations and such?"

"My boss taught me to fake this particular prescription. It's just morphine sulphate. Couldn't afford a doctor every time we had some serious injury on the ranch."

The driver aided Gunderson down off the wagon and up to the porch. He rang the night bell. A minute later a light appeared in an upper window, and shortly the door opened. Ormond heard voices while he lay in pain, dreading every gripping spasm in his midsection.

A few minutes later, Gunderson returned. "Got it." He leaned against the wagon, and the driver boosted him back up. "Told the druggist I had a sick man on the wagon outside. He made me sign for this. We'll split it." He carefully unwrapped a paper packet. Each man took turns licking the powder until it was gone. It tasted slightly bitter, but the sense of taste had almost faded, chased off by the red-hot pinchers gnawing at the stomach.

"You faked the prescription. Maybe the druggist faked the drug. This might not even be morphine."

"It's morphine, all right."

Ormond was convinced when the pains began to ease almost immediately. He relaxed and began to doze. The wagon started again.

Sometime later the wagon stopped. "This is as far as I go, boys."

They were alongside a freight car. The two sick men climbed down and thanked the driver.

"I feel better," Gunderson said. "How about you?"

"Some better."

Leaning on each other, they wobbled toward the porch of a small house in the darkness. By unspoken consent, they lay down on the rough boards. That was the last thing Ormond remembered.

Chapter Nine

When they awoke, it was daylight. The Negro tenants of the shack were up and about but had not disturbed them.

The two men discovered they were beside a railroad track leading to Port Tampa. Wagons were rolling toward the waterfront along with trains of freight cars and flatcars, loaded with troops and cases of sowbelly, beans, and all sorts of canned goods.

Ormond could hardly move or open his eyes. His stomach was as sensitive as if he'd been kicked by a mule.

"Let's go," Gunderson said, pulling him to his feet. They approached a flatcar full of soldiers on a siding. Willing hands reached to help them aboard. An uproar of shouting came from far up the track. A train approached and passed, and they saw the reason for the cheering and waving. Colonel Theodore Roosevelt stood in the open doorway of a boxcar, hands on hips, flashing a toothy grin. The signature blue and white polka dot bandanna of the Rough Riders showed above the khaki uniform that looked as if it'd been slept in. Ormond was proud to be wearing the same kind of blue bandanna while the rest of the army wore red.

The string of flatcars began to move.

"Three to one Roosevelt commandeered that train," Gunderson said. "Opportunistic bastard." But his voice was full of admiration.

"Why do you say that?"

"This whole operation has been chaos from the beginning. No planning, no co-ordination. Too few trains and ships. Supplies late. You think Roosevelt would have his men riding coal hoppers, on a train running in reverse if he had a choice? Not on your life."

"You're right."

"Maybe it's good we got sick. At least we'll arrive aboard ship without being covered with coal dust."

"I think I'd trade ptomaine for coal dust any day," Ormond said, putting a hand to his tender stomach. "Sure could use some warm milk for breakfast."

"Not likely to find any of that around here."

And he didn't. The sandy tent street on the edge of Tampa reeked of chicken frying on spits and other edibles being cooked and sold. But milk was not to be had. Later, Ormond was grateful that he'd followed Gunderson's example and let his empty stomach rest.

In the welter of men and goods crowding the end of the tracks running onto the quay, they located their Company B of the Rough Riders—just in time.

"Fall in! Fall in!" a sergeant yelled. Soot-grimed men scrambled into formation.

"That's our ship a quarter mile down the dock!" the sergeant shouted. "The *Yucatan* . . . the one with number eight painted on her bow. Quick time, march!"

The company stepped off smartly, Ormond and Gunderson in the ranks.

"Company B . . . Double time!"

The Rough Riders broke into a rhythmic trot, horse-collar packs across one shoulder and Krag carbines in hand. They looked as if they could be storming a beach, but they reached the *Yucatan* just behind Company D and, breaking ranks, crowded in a solid stream up the gangway. The Rough Riders had barely reached the main deck when a company of the 71st New York Volunteers arrived on the quay. In the confusion, someone had assigned them to the same ship.

"Roosevelt was first again!" Gunderson said, looking over the rail at the soldiers of the 71st milling on the dock below.

"No wonder we were in such a hurry."

The rush to beat a competing regiment for shipboard space secured them transportation, but didn't hurry their departure. Washington received word that a fleet of Spanish ships was steaming toward the defense of Cuba, so the troop ships were delayed at Tampa while the U.S. Navy went to investigate and intercept.

Day followed sweltering day while the men tried their best to kill time. They practiced manual of arms on deck with Krags that had oily rags stuffed in their muzzles and wrapped around their breeches to prevent salt air corrosion. With nothing to do and plenty of time to do it, discipline was relaxed. Men climbed up and down the mooring lines, swam from ship to ship to visit friends, and did a little fishing—usually without results.

A week later, the Navy decided the Spanish fleet did not exist, and passed down the order to depart for Cuba.

The stubby transports built up steam and, one by one, cast off, plowing down Tampa Bay to the Gulf. Even though they followed one another across the shallow bay, the *Yucatan* somehow veered slightly off course. For a few

frightening minutes it appeared about to ram a vessel an-
chored in the roadstead. At the last second, the helmsman
put the wheel over, steel plates screeching as the ships side-
swiped each other. More damage was done to the reputation of the officer on watch than to the ships.

At sunset, the flotilla dropped anchor outside the harbor
to spend the night.

Next morning dawned bright and clear and the ships got
under way. They set a course down Florida's west coast and
around the tip of the state, aiming for Cuba's northern
shore. Some men speculated whether they would go straight
into Havana harbor and attack the city.

When Ormond and Gunderson posed the question the
second day out, their captain said: "Too heavily defended.
I'm not privy to any high-level strategy, but you can bet
we'll land somewhere a little more vulnerable."

Early on, Ormond and Gunderson found themselves
deck space to spread their blankets. Below decks wooden
plank bunks had been hastily built, four high. But the heat,
lack of ventilation, and darkness made topside space more
desirable.

Unable to boil the lice from their clothing, the men took
to dragging them on a line off the fantail. This worked well
until one of the screws severed the rope and several pairs of
pants and a shirt were lost.

The weather remained good while the convoy steamed
east into the trade winds. Flying fish and porpoises broke
the surface of the sparkling blue Caribbean, chasing the
sluggish convoy. Fresh sea air swept over the men who
lounged in the shade of the superstructure. They were
trying not to think of their hunger and thirst. The food consisted of hardtack and canned hash. The water butts were
four rows of barrels that had been filled some six weeks ear-

lier. Someone had added particles of charcoal for purification.

"From what?" Ormond asked when the sergeant was pointing out the water casks, lashed on the forward deck.

"Whatever was in those barrels before," the sergeant snapped. "Kerosene, pickled fish, you name it."

"It looks like muddy glycerin," Gunderson commented.

"Tastes like bilge water," another man said.

"Don't stand downwind of it, unless you hold your nose."

"That's all we've got to drink till we get to Cuba?" Ormond asked.

"Don't blame me!" the sergeant said, stalking off.

Ormond and Gunderson looked at each other. Gunderson said: "Maybe we can bribe one of the crewmen for some fresh water."

"With what?"

Their new friend, Dismas St. Cyril, came to their rescue. He was aboard the same transport, but didn't see the two men until the first day at sea. Using his artistic talent, he traded sketches of crew members for chicken, vegetables, lemonade, and beer, and was kind enough to share with Ormond and Gunderson. He even smuggled real coffee from the crew's mess. The three men sat, cross-legged, eating their bartered provisions and watching the spectacular sunset. Ormond felt as if they were on some prolonged outing or picnic. He didn't voice his thoughts, because putting to sea signaled the approaching end of the picnic. The serious business of fighting and dying was next on the agenda. The theft of the gold coins from his father, and then from him, the appearance in Prescott of Millard Johnson, their later gun battle with horse thieves, followed by the flight to the military train—all seemed like links in a chain. Each day a new link was forged as they steamed toward the island. He watched men cleaning their weapons and overhauling their gear, men grim and silent, staring off to the south where Cuba lay over the horizon. He knew their thoughts because they were his own. The preparation for war had begun.

C.E. Ormond lowered his copy of the St. Louis *Post-Dispatch* and pulled off his reading glasses as his wife entered the room. "Was that the postman I heard?"

"Yes."

"No word from Millard, I suppose."

"I'm afraid not. Just a few bills. Do you want to see them?"

"No. Just drop them on my desk."

"Anything in the paper?" she asked as she passed his armchair and glanced over his shoulder.

"Nothing but war news, as usual," he said wearily. "The troops have finally shipped out for Cuba." But his mind was not on the war. He sprang up and strode restlessly to the front window where he stood staring out at the big elm in his front yard. The leaves hung limply in the humid June heat. Even with the side windows open and the front and back doors ajar to catch any vagrant draft, he was perspiring in his light cotton dress shirt.

Now he knew that Millard Johnson was not coming back. He should have known better than to trust that Negro. The man had been with him for more than twenty years, but obviously C.E. had never really known him. Last week he'd finally hired a detective to track his son Peter and Millard Johnson. "Probably too little, too late," he muttered aloud to himself, chewing at the corner of his mustache. He'd also sent out a letter to the American

Numismatic Association asking them to notify their members to be on the look-out for his stolen collection. With that many eyes and ears open around the country, someone was bound to spot the unique coins.

Word had somehow been leaked, probably by one of his friends, to the newspaper, and two reporters—one with the UPI—had come to question him about the theft. In hopes of getting free publicity, he'd told them everything, including the descriptions of his son and servant. Officially both of them were now wanted by the law for grand theft. But, with all the other crime in the country, C.E. didn't expect the police to look very hard. Along with his famous luck, hiring a private detective was likely his best hope. But maybe a man was allotted only so much luck in a lifetime. If so, he seemed to have used up his portion.

His stomach burned, but not from hunger, even though it was nearly lunch time. Another dose of soda water would relieve his ulcer. No. He would put it off until bedtime as he always did. He would not surrender to decay until he'd seen his precious collection restored, and those responsible for its theft punished.

Turning away from the window, he shrugged his arms into the galluses that had been hanging at his sides. "Helen!" he called to his wife, "I'm going to the club for a while. Don't bother with supper. I'll get something to eat while I'm out."

A drink or two and some good conversation would improve his mood and relieve the boredom. His personal physician had cautioned him against alcohol because of the ulcer. But C.E. chose to ignore the advice.

He'd long since dismissed his wife's suggestion that perhaps Millard Johnson had met with an accident. C.E. firmly believed that Millard and Peter had split the take and gone their own ways as rich men. But, in order to enjoy their ill-gotten gains, they would have to sell the coins. Then he would likely get word through his network of contacts, and the real chase would begin.

Chapter Ten

"Damn," Ormond breathed, "I'm going to be deaf before I get home."

"*If* you get home," Gunderson said, his voice sounding faint.

Ormond's ears were ringing when the naval bombardment of the Cuban shore suddenly ceased. Navy battleships and cruisers lying three miles offshore had just finished raking artillery fire along the coast near the village of Daiquiri. The ships had also shelled Santiago and Siboney, several miles to the west, a ploy to confuse the Spanish as to where the troops would land.

The crew lowered cargo nets over the side of the *Yucatan*, and men were swarming down into the lifeboats. They tumbled in with their horse-collar packs and carbines, crowding onto the thwarts and in the bottom, twenty or more to the boat, leaving barely enough room for the four sailors to man the oars and the coxswain to swing the tiller.

A delighted Colonel Roosevelt bustled about the deck, supervising the loading. By happy chance, he'd hailed a friend in a steam launch nearby who'd supplied him with a Cuban pilot. The pilot came aboard and guided the troop carrier more than a mile closer to shore, ensuring that the Rough Riders would be among the first to hit the beach.

"By heaven, my men will charge ashore in the first wave!" he cried, leaning over the rail. "That's full enough!" he shouted to the coxswain. "Bring another boat alongside."

Ormond and Gunderson stood in line, awaiting their turn, horse-collar packs and carbines slung across their backs. Ormond shuffled toward the opening in the rail. He admired the skill of the boatmen who bypassed the dilapidated, overcrowded dock and ran their boats through the surf, landing directly on the beach.

The two men climbed and slid down the cargo net without catching a foot, gauged the rise of the boat on the swell, and jumped in. The boat quickly filled, and the sailors pushed away from the side and stroked for shore.

There were no facilities for landing livestock. Farther out, the ship's crews opened side ports in the hulls and shoved out the horses and mules to swim ashore on their own. As Ormond looked, two of the animals turned back toward their ship.

"Their heads are too low in the water," Gunderson said. "They're getting confused because they can't see the shore for the swell."

As he spoke, a bugler on shore sounded "Assembly", followed by "Boots and Saddles". Several of the horses pivoted toward the shore.

"Good idea," Gunderson said. "Those horses are trained to respond to bugle calls."

Boats containing wagon drivers and artillerymen passed

them, rowing toward the struggling animals. They attached halters and lead lines and tied the horses together in strings to lead them to the beach.

"Even so, there'll be a lot of them don't make it," Gunderson said. "What a waste!"

Oars flashed in the sunlight as their boat rose on a swell. Ormond was facing forward and scanned the small village and the green hills beyond it. A blockhouse was visible in a hillside clearing. Palm trees waved above it. There was no sign of life.

"Too damned quiet," he muttered. "Why aren't they opposing our landing?"

"That shelling took the starch out of 'em," Gunderson said, unperturbed.

"But the place looks completely deserted."

"Don't look a gift horse in the mouth."

Some men spoke in low tones. Others sat, gripping the gunwales. As they approached the beach, the surf grew louder. Many of the men from Arizona, possibly natives of the Midwest, had never seen the ocean. The close-up view of breaking waves was a fearful sight to them.

"Good thing we weren't allowed to bring our horses," Gunderson said, looking over his shoulder. "We might have lost them. As it is, there won't be any to spare, that's for sure."

"Poor, dumb brutes. They don't know what this is all about."

"Who does? Don't know about you, but I've just been following the leader."

"Path of least resistance for me. Can't say I joined up for the food or the fancy accommodations."

A commotion and a chorus of shrill cries came from their right. They looked just in time to see a boatload of colored troops capsize. The tall, lean figure of Captain Bucky O'Neill sprinted toward the edge of the pier and dived into the sea, fully clothed. They could see only a flurry of splashing and some swimmers being helped up to the dock. But Ormond could watch for only a few seconds because their own boat rose on a final swell and shot toward the beach on the crest of a breaking wave. The coxswain brought them to a grinding stop on the sand in a lather of foam. A spontaneous cheer went up from the Rough Riders piling out over the sides and the bow.

"Form up! Form up!" a lieutenant shouted. "Knoblauch! Private Herb Knoblauch!"

"Sir?" A broad-shouldered, slim-hipped man stepped forward. Ormond recognized this man he'd met earlier in Tampa. He was a champion athlete and swimmer from New York who was assigned to another company.

"Get over to the dock and report to Captain O'Neill. He wants you to dive for the carbines that were spilled from that boat."

Knoblauch saluted and jogged away. The rest of the men sorted themselves by company as two more boats shot through the surf and landed on the beach.

"Hurry it up! We're sitting ducks on this beach!" Lieutenant Capron yelled. "Right shoulder, arms!" The men scrambled into line disregarding their proper troops. "Forward, march!" They stepped off in ragged formation toward the concealing wall of vegetation.

"Nobody shot at us!" Ormond marveled.

"Hear tell, they was five hundred strong here," a man to his left said. "But they skedaddled even before the ships commenced t'shellin' them."

A hoarse cheer went up from the Arizona contingent of soldiers when they saw the Stars and Stripes, followed by the Rough Rider flag, hoisted on a staff above the red-tiled roof of the blockhouse.

"Quiet in the ranks!" the sergeant yelled. "Move under cover of those trees."

"Always some former regular taking the fun out of everything," the man to Ormond's left complained in an undertone.

Cuban insurgents swarmed out of the brush, grinning and cheering the Rough Riders as they passed.

"Ever see such a ragged bunch of freedom fighters?" Gunderson asked.

Indeed, the *Insurrectos* who greeted them were a crowd of bearded beggars—tattered, thin, brandishing every kind of weapon, from pitchforks and machetes to obsolete muskets and pistols of various makes and calibers. Ormond wiped his brow. If these men were typical of the insurgents, little wonder they hadn't ousted the Spanish rulers.

The majority of the infantry and cavalry were going ashore at Siboney, a dozen miles west of Daiquiri, to confuse the enemy about the location of the main attack. The Rough Riders' objective was the town of Santiago, west of Siboney.

The insurgents convinced the officers that the Spanish had withdrawn toward Siboney. The officers then ordered the Rough Riders to bivouac on a dusty, brush-covered flat near the base of the rugged jungle hills. They had only time to construct shelters of palm fronds and drop their rifles and horse-collar packs before the officers ordered them back to the waterfront to help unload supplies from the ships. Only a few of the pack mules that had survived drowning were available to haul some of the foodstuffs from the waterfront pier to an abandoned warehouse. Most of the hauling was done by streams of men, working like ants.

What had looked so idyllic from shipboard turned out to be a hot, humid, mosquito-filled tropical island, where a little exertion could start streams of sweat. Jacking the sixty-pound boxes from the shore to an empty warehouse 200 yards away turned out to be an exhausting chore. Ormond's dark blue shirt was soaked with perspiration in fifteen minutes. Yet the men kept at their work for several hours.

"I came here to fight the Spanish . . . not to be a stevedore," Gunderson grunted, yanking up yet another case, heaving it to his shoulder. "Glad Saint Cyril got us a good breakfast of ham and eggs and pancakes before we debarked."

"Not so loud," Ormond said, looking around at several of the nearby men. "Sounds like we were given special privileges."

"We were."

"These poor bastards have been surviving on hardtack and canned hash."

"We're damned lucky to have Saint Cyril as our ally. And it didn't cost me anything but an interview."

Ormond nearly dropped his box. "What interview?"

"When he asked me for an interview for his paper, I figured it was the least I could do," the big man said over his shoulder as he trudged ahead.

"What did you tell him? Did you give him our right names?" Ormond was suddenly apprehensive.

"Yeah. Didn't figure it would do any harm."

"My name and Millard Johnson's, too?"

"Yes. The way Saint Cyril talked, I don't know if he'll use any name but mine in his write-up."

"Johnson and I are on the run for a felony," Ormond said in a low voice as they reached the shade of the warehouse and dropped their cases on a growing stack.

"You're a long way from Saint Louis, and we've got more important things to deal with just ahead of us in those hills," Gunderson said with no apologies as he wiped a sleeve across his broad face.

"I wish you hadn't done that, even though we do owe Saint Cyril something for his kindness."

"Tit for tat. Nothing in life is free. Guess I could have asked him to use fake names. But he sketched me, too," Gunderson added. "Good likeness, if I do say so."

"Damn!"

"Don't worry. The chances of your father seeing that piece are at least two million to one. Besides, he doesn't know me."

"You're right," Ormond said, trying to put things into perspective. But the theft of the coins seemed more important at the moment. The closer reality of armed Spanish soldiers was difficult to conjure up since they'd seen no one but the ragged insurgents.

When darkness put an end to the work detail, the men were given permission to break open several cases of canned beef stew and hardtack and stuff their haversacks with whatever they could carry back to their camp. The lack of pack mules was going to be a major problem if the troops moved very far inland.

While they were collecting the canned food, they were besieged by the half-starved insurgents. Many of the men did a good business trading canned sowbelly, hardtack, and corned beef for mangoes, sticks of raw sugar cane, and *plátanos*—large, green bananas with a rough skin. The insurgents eagerly emptied their haversacks made of jute sugar sacks or Pillsbury flour sacks, and stuffed them with American canned goods. It was all a matter of degree. What the Rough Riders looked upon as a nauseating mixture of leftover meat parts were gourmet dinners to these men surviving on what fruit they could find in the jungle and appeasing their appetites with sugar cane.

In any case, the men made trades and each group went away satisfied. The Rough Riders dined on the unfamiliar fruit as a welcome break. "These mangoes have a sweet taste of turpentine," Ormond remarked, making a wry face.

"It's a step down from the good grub Saint Cyril provided us, but better than canned corned beef," Gunderson replied.

Tired as they were from their physical exertion, the Rough Riders did not sleep well in their palm frond shelters that night. The usual rain held off, but rifle blasts awakened the camp several times, sending men scrambling for their weapons.

"Damned green sentries!" Gunderson swore the third time they were awakened. "You'd think they could tell the difference between land crabs scuttling through the leaves and a Spanish patrol."

"First time under fire," Ormond said as if he were a veteran. "Nerves." He returned to his blanket roll but couldn't sleep. He was aware of a heaviness in his stomach, a fear below the surface of consciousness, manifested by a slightly elevated heart rate that did not allow him to relax into sleep. He tried to analyze it, to confront fear and make it retreat. But the more he reflected on it, the more his night imaginings brought forth mental images of being disemboweled by shrapnel from exploding shells. He knew the Spanish soldiers were camped in the hills not many miles away. Just before dark, the westerly breeze had brought the faint sounds of a bugle call to his ears. The enemy was real;

his imaginings were not. Dying quickly from a gunshot to the head did not distress him nearly as much as being horribly mutilated and suffering untold agonies. He'd heard of men having their jaws shot away, rendering them unable to speak or swallow, a mass of blood pouring down their shirts.

The more he tried to put these vivid scenes to rest, the more he tossed and rolled uneasily. He almost welcomed the next alarm as a sentry, in spite of himself and the warnings of his officers, blazed away in the darkness at the attacking land crabs.

The next morning Ormond was feeling dragged out and listless, running on reserves of energy. The physical labor and lying sleepless on the hard ground had taken their toll. He was so hungry even the corned beef hash, hardtack, and coffee were palatable. He had three cups of coffee, then chewed on a shaving of sugar cane for energy. Fortunately confusion and delay were again the regimen of the first half day. Then, when the men were cooking food for the midday meal, the order was passed to fall into ranks with rifles, ammunition belts, and horse-collar packs.

"Fall in! On the double!"

"What's the big rush all of a sudden, Sarge?" one of the men griped, gnawing on a strip of limp sowbelly.

The sergeant grabbed the coffee pot and sloshed its contents onto the fire, hissing steam obscuring the non-com. "Just move your lazy carcass!"

As the sergeant turned away, someone said under his breath: "Hell, a couple weeks ago, he was one of us. Now, you'd think he was Gawd Awmighty."

Captain McClintock came striding among the palm shelters and announced: "General Wheeler has ordered us to march on Siboney. If the Spanish haven't retreated from their position by the time we get there, we're to run 'em out and secure the area."

"I thought the regular infantry landed there," Gunderson said.

"The generals don't consult me on strategy," the captain said, moving on.

"How far?" Ormond asked the surly sergeant.

"You just keep pickin 'em up and layin 'em down and you'll be there afore ya know it," he said.

"About nine miles," another man answered.

Fifteen minutes later, Company B swung into fours abreast and marched off along the trail. The early afternoon humidity quickly drained their energy.

"At least we're not marching uphill," Ormond panted.

"Only about half the time," Gunderson said.

Hundreds of marching feet churned up clouds of dust. The tropical sun bore down and the foliage blocked the sea breeze. Their burdens grew heavier, and soon the soldiers began discarding non-essential items such as canned corned beef to join other things cast aside by the weary marchers ahead of them. Breath came short and sweat stung the eyes. The eight-pound carbines became twenty. Canteens were drained. The four abreast formation thinned to two, then, before half the distance was covered, the column straggled out in a loose single file. Colonel Leonard Wood rode at the head of the column, and Colonel Roosevelt led his own brigade on Little Texas, the only horse of his to survive the trip. The bespectacled colonel rode back along the trail, urging the men on. "Close ranks, boys! It's not much farther. Buck up!"

Ormond thought how ridiculous this sounded from a man on horseback.

"This is more than I've walked my whole life!" a bowlegged cowboy snorted, blowing dust out of his nose.

Another lanky trooper sat at the side of the trail, head drooping.

"Where you from, soldier?" Roosevelt asked, reining up his mount.

"Portales, Arizona, sir."

"Originally?"

"Alabama."

"Then Fighting Joe Wheeler's your man. He's an ex-Confederate, and spitting fire to get after those Spaniards he's spotted. You can be one of the first to follow him and give them a licking. But you have to get off your butt and get down the trail to Siboney."

Roosevelt wheeled his horse and dashed away as the soldier used his carbine for a crutch and pushed himself to his feet.

The troops filtered into the squalid hamlet of Siboney after dark and began dividing up to form messes and find shelter as best they could.

"If only the Spaniards could see us now," Gunderson said, gathering some dry brush in the dark. "One strong attack would wipe us all out."

"They're probably as disorganized as we are." Ormond was trying to convince himself.

Big drops of rain began to spatter around them.

"Here comes one of those tropical downpours!" Gunderson said.

Ormond threw what he could onto his blanket and snatched it up. "Quick . . . bring that firewood and duck under those wrecked railroad cars."

In thirty minutes, the two men had a fire going and were brewing a pot of coffee for themselves and anyone who wanted to huddle around in their semi-dry shelter to share it with them. There was no thought of unit or company division.

The glare of naval searchlights in the distance aided the debarkation of the 1st Division, which continued in the rain.

Wrapped in his blanket on the soft sand of the railroad embankment, Ormond went to sleep to the sound of rain drumming on the wrecked boxcars that were tilted outward to form their shelter. It was almost like being at home—wherever home was.

Chapter Eleven

Peter Ormond dreamed the dark-haired woman who'd picked his pocket of the gold coins was coming back to return them. With a great sense of relief he reached for the coins in their original wooden strips as she slowly, reluctantly held them out to him. He didn't want to break the spell by asking her why she'd had a change of heart. Instead, he showed her the remaining coins belonging to his father and told her how glad he was to get them all back to return to their rightful owner. Suddenly her male accomplice appeared and snatched the six remaining coins from Ormond's hand. The two then turned and leaped aboard a moving train. Ormond tried to run after them but his legs were heavy. He yelled at them to stop.

"Peter! Wake up!" A hand was shaking him. He opened his gritty eyes a slit. "Huh?"

"You OK? You were hollering in your sleep." It was Gunderson's voice.

The woman wasn't there? It took several seconds for Ormond to tear himself loose from the vivid nightmare, to separate that scene from reality.

He groaned and rolled over, pushing himself to a sitting position. "A bad dream," he muttered, noting the foul taste in his dry mouth. His surroundings came back to him, and he almost wished he had not awakened.

"Come on, get up. Didn't you hear 'Reveille'?"

Ormond poured some water from the canteen into his cupped hand and rubbed his eyes, wiping his face with a shirt sleeve. He sprinkled water on his tangled hair and ran a pocket comb through it.

Gunderson had risen early. Now he stirred up the fire and put on the frying pan and coffee pot. "Have some sowbelly and coffee."

In spite of his dream, Ormond had slept soundly, mostly from exhaustion and lack of sleep the night before.

The camp was coming to life, and smoke from cook fires rose into the windless air. The rain was gone and the first rays of sun slanted over the trees, creating sparkling diamonds from drops of moisture on the bushes.

He poured himself a cup of coffee. His stomach could face no food. He thought of what might lie ahead and was amazed at the tension in his body. His bowels began to cramp and he hurriedly disappeared behind some shrubbery at the end of an overturned boxcar.

A few minutes later, he felt relieved, but the dread still hung heavily in his lower belly, a continuous nausea, the way fear always manifested itself to him. He pulled up his galluses and kneeled to lace up his canvas leggings.

Five minutes later, the order came to fall in with rifles and canteens. Everything else was to be left behind.

"Looks like serious business this time," Gunderson said, buckling on his webbed ammunition belt. "At least we won't have to carry all our gear."

"Cancel that order!" the sergeant yelled. "The captain

says to bring all your stuff."

"What?"

"You heard me . . . pack the ends of those blanket rolls . . . canned meat, green coffee beans, hardtack, canned tomatoes, frying pan . . . the works."

"We gonna be camping or fighting, Sarg?"

"Probably both. In any case, we won't be back this way, so bring it all."

They filled their canvas-covered canteens and slung them from their shoulders on long straps. Besides the carbines and full ammunition belts, the blanket roll with canned goods weighted down each man.

Once the companies were formed, Colonel Roosevelt addressed the men, walking up and down, projecting his voice to be heard.

"I wouldn't ask any man to go into action without telling him what he's up against." He cleared his throat and ran his gaze down the ranks. "General Wheeler has ordered us to attack the Spanish who were last reported in the hills near Sevilla, a few miles from here. General Young will lead his column of regulars up the valley just east of us, while the Rough Riders will march on a trail roughly parallel. We will rendezvous at a crossroads near Sevilla." He paused, facing them, hands clasped behind his back, campaign hat squarely on his head. His tailor-made khaki uniform was more wrinkled than ever. "Colonel Leonard Wood will lead us on horseback, and I will ride in front of the first company with Major Brodie and Captain McClintock. The Arizona troops of Captains Capron, Haston, and Muller will follow. Colonel Wood will set a fast pace because the regulars have an easier road and will make better time. Both our columns must arrive simultaneously." He pushed up the wire-rimmed spectacles more securely on his nose and gave the soldiers a searching look. "OK, men, let's show 'em what the First Volunteer Cavalry is made of. Move out!"

Roosevelt mounted his horse and trotted to the head of the column while Major Brodie and the company officers relayed orders to the sergeants. The men stepped off smartly on command, accoutrements rattling.

The air was cool, but damp. Ormond felt stiff from the nine-mile march of the day before. But he worked that out in the first twenty minutes. The trail wound away from the coast, up toward the top of a ridge, quickly growing so narrow that the men had to string out, single file. Thick growth lined both sides of the trail like tangled green walls, so they couldn't deploy flankers. Captain Capron sent Sergeant Hamilton Fish and three men out front on point. Twenty more followed some distance back. Then came Capron's troop, followed by Colonel Wood and Colonel Roosevelt and the three troops of his squadron. One of the three was Captain McClintock's Company B with Ormond and Gunderson.

Roosevelt rode back along the marching column. A few minutes later he returned and edged his mount alongside Wood, tossing him a quick salute. "Due respect, Colonel, but I think we're pushing the men a little too fast. A lot of them are dropping their packs or falling out. I suggest a short rest stop."

These words fell like a cooling mist on Ormond. He was soaked with sweat, breathing hard. But his hopes were dashed a second later when Wood said: "We can't stop, or even slow down. We must be there when the regulars arrive. The men will have to keep up as best they can."

"Yes, sir!" Roosevelt wheeled his horse and forced his way carefully back along the narrow trail to urge the stragglers to greater effort.

The morning sun topped the trees and its rays sparkled off the carbine barrels, tin cups, buckles, brass cartridges, and 1st Volunteer Cavalry insignias pinned to hats. The sun also sucked the moisture out of the shambling, rattling column.

Ormond, fearful earlier, was now calmer, finding it difficult to realize this march was something more than just another training exercise. He'd never seen a tropical rain forest and looked at the palms and curiously flat-topped trees. He admired a mass of brilliant scarlet flowers and soaked up the beauty around him without knowing the names of any of the plants. Strange screeches, cries, and coos surrounded them on all sides as a variety of birds greeted the day.

In spite of repeated warnings from the officers, the men talked and joked, as if this were a Sunday hunting excursion. Ormond became aware of a conversation between two men behind him. "Randy Neely was the best damned cowhand I ever worked with," one of them said. "But he allowed there warn't no future in it, and he wanted somethin' permanent, so maybe he could afford to get hitched and settle down. Went over to Silver City, New Mexico and started a saloon."

"Saloon?" the other man said. "Wish I had a cold beer right about now."

"I would imagine there's plenty of beer in Santiago, where we're headed," a familiar, cultured voice said. "And you'll probably be there in time to have some tomorrow."

Ormond jerked his gaze up from the ground in front and saw Dismas St. Cyril. The artist pushed along the edge of the narrow trail, working his way toward the head of the column. His wide-brimmed hat was set at a jaunty angle and his flat bag with sketchbook and writing materials swung from one shoulder, Army canteen from the other. His lean form swung up the steep trail. He hardly seemed out of breath, even though perspiration was coursing down his face.

Ormond and Gunderson grinned at each other. It was good to have the devil-may-care artist and reporter with them.

"Where's Richard Harding Davis?" Gunderson asked. "I didn't think he'd miss this."

"Oh, the socialite reporter is on up ahead near the point. He somehow managed to wangle a horse to ride." Then he winked. "Overweight, middle-aged men need all the help they can get."

"You're not armed," Ormond said.

"I didn't come to fight. I came to observe and record."

"You want my Bisley, just in case?" The weapon and an extra bag of .32 ammunition were growing heavier on his hip with every step. Each of the other Rough Riders carried the issue Colt .45 with fifty cartridges.

"No, thanks. I'll keep my head down," St. Cyril said. "No heavy weapons for me." Unencumbered, except for the canteen, paper, and pens, he moved quickly past the plodding column.

They crested the ridge above Siboney and the trail descended toward Sevilla. The Rough Riders began to make better time. Relieved chatter filled the ranks. Some of the men in the rear of Company B even struck up a ragged chorus of "There'll Be a Hot Time in the Old Town Tonight".

Ormond didn't join in, but the lively air gave him a lift. His feet didn't feel so heavy. He hitched up his sagging belt of .30-40 Krag cartridges and picked up the pace. It was good to get a second wind. He was in better condition than he'd thought.

They marched for another hour. By then thirst had become more of a concern than the rumored Spanish.

The column came to a sudden halt. Ormond uncorked his canteen and took four large gulps to soothe his burning throat. He would have drunk the whole thing but didn't know how long he'd have to make the tepid water last.

Colonel Wood sent word back along the line that the advance guard had come upon a Spanish outpost. "Fill magazines!" The command rippled down the column. There was a general metallic clacking and ratcheting as dozens of men flipped open the loading gates on the right sides of their Krag carbines and dropped in five loose shells.

Ormond fumbled to extract bottle-nosed cartridges from his belt loops. He fingered a cool brass cartridge the size of his ring finger, realizing it held the power of life and death over another human. And not far away in that jungle was someone who had the same power over him. Looking at the faces around him, he wondered if he were the only one reflecting on such things. Most of the men seemed unconcerned, still chatting casually.

A lieutenant rode up and saluted Roosevelt. "Colonel Wood's orders, sir. Deploy three troops to the right of the trail. Colonel Brodie will deploy two troops to the left. Advance until you engage the enemy. One troop will be held in reserve."

Roosevelt wheeled his horse. "Troops A, B, and G to the right. L Troop remain on the trail."

Shouted orders followed from the company officers.

"Drop your packs, men, and follow me!" Captain McClintock cried.

The Rough Riders shrugged out of their horse-collar packs and plunged into the thick jungle, on the heels of Captains McClintock and Bucky O'Neill.

Almost immediately the dense growth raked through the ranks, separating the men. Gunfire came from up ahead. Ormond held his Krag and stumbled down a slope congested with brush and vines toward the valley road the regulars had marched on. Gunderson was beside him, and then he wasn't, disappearing into the greenery a few yards away. More gunfire cracked up ahead and Mauser bullets sang through the trees, humming like telephone wires. The smokeless powder and the undergrowth concealed the source of fire. Several Rough Riders shot back at the unseen enemy.

Ormond's heart hammered in his chest and breath came in short gasps. Sweat stung his eyes. The fire seemed to come from the hillside across the narrow valley, maybe 500 yards away. The Spanish were shooting high and blind, their slugs clipping leaves and twigs overhead.

"Ahhh!" A Rough Rider dropped his weapon and fell with a grunt.

Ormond paused, panting, and stared at Harry Heffner of G Troop. A red stain was spreading over the man's khaki pants near his hips. Ormond felt saliva rush into his mouth from sudden nausea.

The wounded man looked up. Their gazes locked. "Can't move my legs," he gasped. "Prop me behind that tree."

Without thinking, Ormond sprang to obey. Having something immediate to do helped quell his surging panic. His knees trembled from excitement as he gripped Heffner's shoulders and began dragging him toward the base of a tall palm. Another soldier stopped to help.

Heffner gritted his teeth as each man grabbed an arm and struggled to move his dead weight. "Don't worry about hurting me. It's mostly numb. Just leave me a canteen and my rifle."

They did as requested. Before moving on, Ormond and the other soldier exchanged a glance that said: *This man knows he's done for, but he has the courage to continue fighting to his last breath.*

"Can't see nothing to shoot at," the other Rough Rider said. He slowly swung the barrel of his carbine. "Now and again I get a glimpse of some red-tiled buildings about a quarter mile thataway. Might be holed up there."

Ormond remained silent, fighting his rising panic, and allowed the other man to disappear ahead of him.

Another fusillade of bullets zipped through the foliage above his head, but this time closer. The Spaniards were getting the range.

About eighty yards away the sun shone through a break in the trees where a loose line of infantry moved up the road, firing to their right. They were fully exposed, and puffs of smoke from their black powder rifles gave the Spanish additional targets. Two mules with Colt machine-guns strapped to their pack saddles began to buck and jump. Despite the profane efforts of the mule handlers, the animals panicked at the gunfire, jerking their lead lines loose and galloped back down the road.

Ormond forced his legs to move forward. He was alone now. To his right and left, a few blue-shirted forms crashed through the undergrowth, intent on closing with the enemy. The staccato cracking of Mausers increased, and suddenly a man coming up behind Ormond plunged forward on his face. Ormond jumped and turned to see the man's hat roll away. The back of his head was a mass of blood where the bullet had crashed through.

Gripped with fear, Ormond could hardly get his breath. The sight of sudden death released his panic. He turned and ran, dropping his Krag. The instinct for self-preservation overcame everything else, and he ran blindly away from the gunfire. *What if they find my body with a bullet hole in the back? They'll know I ran.* This was his only thought as his body fled from the danger without his consciously willing it to do so. Stumbling, falling, tearing the skin of his hands and knees on thorns and roots, he lost all sense of time or distance. Shadowy figures flowed past, going the other way. Someone shouted at him, but he ignored everything, gripped by a compulsion to escape those deadly bullets that were flying like horizontal hail through the trees. Completely out of control, his legs carried him faster than he'd ever run before. Branches and leaves whipped at his face, snatching off his hat.

Finally his burning lungs could no longer keep up with the demands of his legs. He slowed to a stop, hands on knees, oblivious to everything as he sucked in great draughts of the humid air. Then he wilted, face down, onto the leaf mold of the jungle floor, heedless of any centipedes, other insects, or snakes.

For at least fifteen minutes he lay there, nauseated, wondering if he would die of exhaustion. But it was not to be. He gradually began to rebound. His labored breathing and racing heart slowly subsided. He became conscious of his surroundings, and listened for sounds of battle. Above the screeching birdcalls he could barely make out a distant popping of rifle fire. His rush of adrenaline ebbed, leaving him weak as he came back from his dream-like state.

Rolling over in the vegetation, he stared up at the leafy canopy overhead. Blue sky blinked through in only a few spots. He pushed up to a sitting position, becoming aware of the stinging cuts on his hands. Sweat soaked his blue shirt and torn khaki pants. His mouth and throat were dry and he reached for his canteen. But it was gone. The webbed cartridge belt was still buckled around his waist, and from it was suspended the holstered Bisley. He felt the lumps of loose, .32 ammunition in his pants pocket.

He climbed to his feet and took a deep breath. The realization of what he'd done crept into his consciousness. The cuts and bruises were as nothing compared to the shame and remorse that enveloped him. He'd panicked and run away in the face of danger. This single, indisputable fact clamped onto his mind and refused to go away. He could imagine a scarlet C for coward emblazoned on his forehead.

But it wasn't his fault. Fear and panic had seized him, and taken control of his body against his will. A weak excuse at best. *You showed the white feather. You turned tail and skedaddled. Your yellow streak is showing.* He could hear the ridicule now. Or they would simply look at him and turn away, silently ignoring him as if he no longer existed.

Others had slipped away. He remembered seeing one or two sitting on the ground, apparently unhurt, waiting for the clash to end. If anyone had noticed, these men would get the same treatment. They would all be tarred with the same black brush. But he, Peter Ormond, had openly run away. There could be no doubt about his intentions. He would be a pariah, a useless excuse for a man. The fact that he might be court-martialed for cowardice in the face of the enemy was only a minor inconvenience compared to the public ridicule he would face.

He blinked away the hot tears that welled up in his eyes. He was finally exposed for what he knew himself to be. Ever since he was eleven and had allowed himself to be beaten up by a neighborhood bully, he'd suspected he was a coward. Until now, he'd managed to cover it up with various subterfuges. Now he'd exposed his innermost failing for all to see. He couldn't blame his father—although the old man's ridicule had aggravated his character deficiency. He couldn't even claim bravery for stealing his father's coins. Armed robbery was a brave act; sneak thievery was cowardly. A leopard could not change his spots. Why in the world had he ever joined the Army? It was the force of circumstance after they'd boarded the train to escape the rustlers. At the time, it seemed the logical thing to do—a chance for a new beginning. He'd never thought ahead about how he might react in combat. The running fight in the darkness with the rustlers had happened so fast, he'd had no time to be afraid. Only later had he been a little shaky.

He began to walk aimlessly in the general direction of the coast and tried to find something positive in himself. Hadn't God put the instinct for self-preservation in all men? Whose idea was this bravery business, anyway? Some Indian tribes, including the fearsome Apaches, attached no shame to running away if the odds didn't favor victory. Bravery was a European white man's concept—deliberately overcoming natural impulses to put oneself in mortal danger, for whatever purpose. He had obeyed his natural instinct. That might be a good philosophical argument, but he was a prisoner of his culture and could not escape its dictates.

He dreaded the ridicule. Maybe if he kept silent no one would say anything. Had anyone witnessed his inglorious retreat? He could feel his face burning. How could he face Gunderson or any other Rough Rider? He could always lie, and pretend some urgent problem had sent him to the rear. Food poisoning, maybe.

But he couldn't lie. He could not compound his first offense with a second. He thought briefly of deserting. But he was on an island and had nowhere to go. He couldn't even speak Spanish.

He stopped, the weight of the universe crushing his shoulders. He wished he were dead and done with it all.

A flash of white caught his eye. His heart gave a leap as he reached for his pistol. A man in a bloody white shirt sagged against a tree trunk 100 feet away. It was not a uniform he knew—probably a Cuban insurgent. He crept toward the injured man, pistol drawn.

The man raised his head and stared at him. It was Dismas St. Cyril!

Chapter Twelve

"*Ahh*, Peter Ormond! What a stroke of luck." With an obvious effort, the reporter pushed himself erect.

"You hit bad?" Self-pitying thoughts vanished as he sprang to St. Cyril's side.

"Not fatal, I hope. Got two holes for the price of one."

"What?"

St. Cyril pulled open his torn shirt and pointed. "In here . . . out there." Two small holes in his abdomen were connected by a six-inch purple welt. "Lucky I was standing sideways and hadn't eaten any lunch." He forced a grin. "Feel up to helping me to the rear where I can get this mosquito bite treated before it festers?"

"Here, lean on me." Ormond slid an arm around the lean man and pulled him away from the tree.

"Whoa!" St. Cyril reeled slightly. "As a Southern friend of mine would say, I feel plumb swimmy-headed." He was pale and sweaty. Ormond supported most of St. Cyril's weight as the reporter's legs were wobbly.

"Probably shock and loss of blood," Ormond said, getting a better grip, although he noted that not much blood had leaked onto the shirt front.

"Plus a malarial attack," St. Cyril said, taking a long, shuddering breath. "Those pesky little parasites been multiplying in my red blood cells. Decided this was the time to bust out all at once. Caused the chills and fever."

"Where'd you pick up malaria?"

"Spent a few weeks in Central America about ten years ago."

"Got any quinine?"

St. Cyril shook his head. "Nope. Never carry it. Wishful thinking, I suppose. Keep hoping I'll outlive this damned stuff. But once it gets hold of you, it won't let go."

"Which way?"

St. Cyril inclined his head. "Straight that way. We aren't too far off the trail."

They shuffled through the dry palmetto fronds without talking until they abruptly broke free of the jungle growth onto the trampled path.

"Let's rest here a minute." St. Cyril sagged to the ground.

Ormond lowered himself to one knee beside him and steadied the reporter's hand as he tipped up his canteen.

"Where were you?" Ormond asked.

"Well, Sergeant Hamilton Fish and two men were on the point. I was with several others a short way back." He attempted a smile. "Couldn't let Richard Harding Davis scoop me on the first action."

"What happened?"

He shrugged. "We walked into an ambush . . . like the bunch of amateurs we are. The Spanish let go at us from both sides of the trail. Sergeant Fish took a bullet in the head. Probably a half dozen killed, and as many more wounded." He snorted his disgust. "Too much swagger and not enough caution. I was hit but managed to get down and crawl away through the brush. I can write an account of what I saw and heard, but it was pretty confusing." St. Cyril corked the canteen and nodded toward the distant boom of artillery. "Things get hot up there after I left?"

An evasion leaped to his lips, but then Ormond hesitated. If he were ever to admit his cowardice, it would be to this unconventional man. "Don't know," he said. "I ran as soon as the shooting got close."

St. Cyril's eyes focused on him with keen interest. "Tell me about it."

Ormond looked away and took a deep breath. Then he proceeded to explain, as best he could, what he'd done. It was a phenomenon he didn't really understand. He could feel his face reddening as he forced himself to tell exactly what had occurred, making no excuses for his behavior. When he finished, he waited for St. Cyril's disapproval or, at least, his pity. He got neither.

"By God!" the reporter exclaimed, pulling a silver flask from a hip pocket. "A man with guts who thinks for himself! Have a drink." He held out the flask.

Ormond took a swig. The fiery brandy warmed him. He had another, the fumes clearing his stuffy nose.

Taking the flask, St. Cyril saluted him silently with it and treated himself to a swallow. He coughed, but his pale face gradually began to regain a little color.

"I'm ashamed," Ormond said quietly. "I seemed to have no control of myself." He stopped talking as two soldiers hurried along the trail, bearing a wounded man on a litter. They passed quickly out of sight.

"That man looked a lot worse off than I am," St. Cyril said. "Let's go."

They continued downhill toward the field hospital near Siboney, but managed only 200 yards before St. Cyril had to stop and rest once more.

"You don't need an excuse for self-preservation," he said, sipping at the brandy again. "But, if anyone asks or accuses . . . you stopped to help me."

Ormond could feel his face flushing again. "Thanks, but I'll take my dose of medicine, no matter how bitter it might be. I may not have the courage to face the Spanish guns, but at least I have the courage to admit it."

" 'Better a live mouse than a dead lion.' Is that from the Psalms? Can't recall." Then the reporter added: "Sorry. Didn't mean to refer to you as a mouse. But there's a lot to be said for being alive . . . under any circumstances." He paused to examine the drying blood on his shirt front. "I have no stomach for all that. In the interest of doing my job, I got a little closer to the fray than I intended."

Ormond licked his dry lips, wondering if St. Cyril might share a little water. But he kept silent.

"I'm an agnostic," the reporter continued, "but I value human existence. Who knows? It may be the only life we have. Some of those fools . . ."—he jerked his head toward the ridge—"will never live to see the sunset. And for what? Some cause greater than themselves? To make the world a better place by forcing some perceived evil back into its hole?" He snorted a derisive laugh. "History is rife with wars, justified in every generation by somebody's idea of a noble cause. In this case it's to protect the sugar interests, or to keep the Spanish power farther off our coast."

They fell silent for several seconds and Ormond realized the sounds of distant conflict had ceased. The short battle was over. A mounted courier came galloping down the trail and disappeared in a swirl of dust.

"Why did you come here?" Ormond said.

"I might ask the same of you," St. Cyril replied. "My

newspaper offered me a bonus if I followed the troops and scooped the Hearst reporters with exclusive interviews, and spiced them up with details of battle. The simple answer is . . . I needed the money. My wife has chronic health problems and our three children are all under twelve. I'm heavily insured, in case I don't return." He smiled ruefully. "A situation where I'm worth more dead than alive."

Ormond confided what had led to his own enlistment. He included the theft of the gold coins—a fact that he was afraid to admit to others. But he freely told the story to St. Cyril as he would have to a kindly, non-judgmental priest.

They struggled to their feet, and proceeded at a slow walk. St. Cyril seemed able to bear most of his own weight, but stayed slightly stooped, pressing a clean handkerchief to his abdominal wound. This time they made a quarter mile before the reporter had to rest.

"Thanks for helping me," St. Cyril said. "If you hadn't come along, I might have laid out there and died."

"I don't think your wound is mortal," Ormond said to deflect the embarrassing expression of gratitude.

"Beside the point. Ever stop to wonder why men will scratch and claw and suffer and die to save one individual while dozens are dying around them?" He arched his fine eyebrows over the aquiline nose.

Ormond shook his head.

"It's not as if one man is going to mean much to the survival of the species, or because his rescuers have computed how much more work he can contribute to society. No. It's because each person has within him, or her, a whole universe. It's not a matter of saving one out of a colony of ants. The saving of one human is the saving of an empire whose significance can't be compared with anything else." He looked intently at Ormond who sat on the ground next to

169

him. "Inside this one skull . . ."—he tapped his own head—"lives a world. Parents, friends, a home, hot soup on the table, songs sung in a saloon, loving kindness and anger, perhaps social consciousness. But who can measure the value of one man? Our ancestors drew antelope on cave walls. Thousands of years later, that gesture still radiates through us. Man's gestures are an eternal spring. We'll go to extraordinary lengths to save one man even while hundreds are dying in a plague or being killed in war. Not good cost accounting . . . until you realize that one man may be solitary . . . but he is also universal." St. Cyril paused to catch his breath, and wipe his pale, clammy face.

" 'Therefore, never send to know for whom the bell tolls. It tolls for thee,' " Ormond muttered.

"Exactly. Nice to know you've read John Donne." St. Cyril thrust out a hand to be helped up.

The two men scuffed along the dusty trail.

"A man must follow his conscience or his instincts, or he's something less than a man," St. Cyril said. "Whether you're praised or blamed for your actions today doesn't matter at all. In a few short years we'll all be under the sod . . . you, and I and that bunch of so-called heroes out there. Death is the great leveler . . . heroes or goats, famous or notorious, we'll all be forgotten." His face creased in a wry smile. "As my favorite barroom philosopher, Mister Dooley, says . . . 'What's fame, after all, me lad? 'Tis as apt to be what someone writes on your tombstone.' "

Chapter Thirteen

"Uuhhh!" St. Cyril grimaced in pain, sweat trickling down his blanched face.

"Figured it would sting a little." A soldier assisting the regimental surgeon pulled the Krag cleaning rod out of the wound in the reporter's abdomen. Then he shoved it back in, following the bullet's path below the surface until the blood-soaked patch of lint appeared at the exit wound. "Gotta make sure the tunnel is cleaned free of foreign matter." The man was clearly not interested in the reporter's distress.

"Shit!" St. Cyril gasped while the volunteer thrust and yanked the rod in the wound as if cleaning the barrel of a gun. The six-inch purple welt connecting the two holes looked dark and angry.

St. Cyril clenched his fists. "It didn't hurt this bad when the bullet went through."

The amateur nurse tucked a small, medicine-soaked patch of cloth into each hole, then wiped the skin clean with a wad of cotton. "There ya go. Good as new." He got up and went to help with another wounded man.

To Ormond, the field hospital, set up under two

open-sided tents near Siboney, was mass confusion. Walking wounded were continuously arriving, as well as the severely injured on litters.

Ormond helped St. Cyril to a shady spot under a palm outside and away from the odors of chloroform, alcohol, and feces. The welcome trade winds dried the perspiration on their faces and carried the stench clear of them.

St. Cyril medicated himself with a swig of brandy from his pocket flask. "I'm mighty lucky," he said. "Ed Marshal got hit in the spine."

"Who?" Ormond was looking around for anyone from his troop who might have witnessed his hasty departure.

"Reporter for the New York *Journal.* It's a Hearst paper."

"Kill him?"

"Not yet. He's being worked on over there. Nice guy, but not too smart. He was wearing a long, white cotton coat. Maybe thought it would be cooler in the tropics, or it would identify him as a non-combatant." He shook his head. "All it did was make him a better target. Some sniper probably figures he got himself a high-ranking officer."

Surgeons in bloody aprons worked quickly on the wounded atop makeshift tables. Ormond looked away from the sickening sight and tried to shut his ears to the groans and cries. He took a deep breath of fresh air and rested his eyes on the tranquil blue Caribbean.

"I'll be damned!"

"What?" Ormond jerked his attention back.

"There's old Willie himself!"

"Willie?"

"William Randolph Hearst."

"Where?"

St. Cyril pointed weakly. "On the horse."

In spite of the heat, the big man wore a dark suit, white shirt, and straight-brimmed gray hat. He was observing the battle-weary troops filtering back to the field hospital. Attending him were three young men, one of them busy setting up a folding table and portable typewriter. Another had spread a white canvas ground cover and was unpacking a picnic lunch with various delicacies.

"Roughing it," commented St. Cyril. "And you can bet his employees will hear about it if things aren't done to his satisfaction."

The two watched Hearst for several minutes until everything was in readiness, and he dismounted, handing his horse's reins to a minion.

"I've got to get a little closer and see what he's doing," St. Cyril said, struggling to his feet.

Ormond helped him and they casually moved toward the newspaper magnate's entourage. Hearst was leaning back in a canvas camp chair, hat on the ground beside him. His sandy hair, slightly beaked nose, and light, hooded eyes gave him a hawk-like appearance. He was sampling a sandwich and dictating to a young man in a stiff collar at the typewriter.

"The Rough Riders have met and bloodied the Spaniards at Las Guasimas where the cowardly. . . ."

"Sir, how do you spell Las Guasimas?" the typist interrupted.

"How the hell should I know?" Hearst snapped. "I don't speak that heathen lingo. Now . . . where was I? Ah, yes, . . . outnumbered five to one, the Rough Riders, sabers flashing, attacked the Spanish barbarians who were entrenched in jungle blockhouses. . . ."

"They didn't have any sabers, sir."

"I saw Roosevelt with one."

173

"He threw it away. The Rough Riders were using Krags," an aide corrected him.

"Shouting . . . 'Remember the *Maine*!' the rawhide-tough Westerners whipped their mounts into the very mouths of the roaring cannon. . . ."

"They were on foot, sir."

Hearst shot the impertinent aide a withering look. "I didn't sell enough papers to build an empire by reporting dry facts!"

He crossed his legs and leaned back, staring off into space, apparently organizing his thoughts, then resumed dictating. The Remington portable clattered away as fast as the clerk could type.

Ormond listened in amazement as Hearst turned the skirmish into a major battle, embellished with purple prose.

"Lying son-of-a-bitch!" St. Cyril hissed, his face quickly regaining its color. "Why doesn't he report that the Rough Riders were ambushed and had at least eight men killed and several more wounded? He's the one man most responsible for fanning the spark of the *Maine* accident into a full-scale war."

"Accident? So you don't believe the Spanish blew up that ship?" Ormond asked quietly, trying to guide the wounded man out of hearing range.

"Why would they? They had nothing to gain by it. They knew Roosevelt, as Assistant Secretary of the Navy, was agitating for war, and that such an act as sabotaging the *Maine* would only infuriate the Americans."

"Well, that's all past history. We're in the middle of it now."

St. Cyril didn't answer as he had his flask tipped up.

"Let me get you a blanket to rest on and I'll go find us

something to eat," Ormond said, thinking St. Cyril was sounding more like an irate politician than a cool-headed philosopher.

Ormond wandered toward the waterfront. No food was being served. A few men were snacking from their haversacks. He wondered what had become of Millard Johnson and the Buzzacot oven. He would have welcomed a good meal right now. Gunderson was still in the jungle on the ridge, hopefully unhurt, probably with their Company B. From snatches of conversation he overheard, Ormond knew the Spanish had abandoned their entrenched positions and retreated toward Santiago, leaving the Americans in possession of the field and several isolated blockhouses. Lieutenant Allyn Capron had been killed and Captain McClintock of B Company had taken two bullets in his lower leg. Even Major Brodie had been hit in the wrist. Estimates were about twenty killed and twice that number wounded.

As he passed among the less seriously wounded, Ormond sensed that most of them were averting their eyes from him.

"Hey, Ormond!" It was Henry Tompkins, a soldier from his own Company B, sitting on the ground with his arm in a sling.

Ormond started. "Yeah?"

"Did you go off with Sergeant Hughes's squad? I didn't see you."

"Uh . . . no. Why?"

"Heard he took his squad down a wrong trail and got lost. They had to fight all by themselves."

"Wasn't with them."

"Where you hit?" the man asked. "I took one through the fleshy part of my arm. When they come to check me, I had a slug in the butt I didn't even feel at first till they got to probing around for it." He sounded almost ecstatic with relief and wanted to talk. "Bad place to get shot. Somebody might think I was running."

"Gotta go," Ormond muttered.

"The rest of the troop is still up yonder. Wish I was with 'em. Believe I got me one of them spics, but I ain't sure."

Ormond eased away while the man rambled on. 100 yards farther, he found a huge pile of supplies, stacked haphazardly. Boxes of canned meat, tomatoes, and beans were in evidence. A case of beef stew had been broken open, and, since no one was around, he helped himself. He jimmied open the top with his sheath knife and stabbed a few pieces of the flabby meat. It was a testament to his hunger that the beef actually tasted good. He finished the can and drank the thin gravy. Then he loaded his pockets with three more cans and grabbed a small, unopened box of hardtack.

While the reporter ate, litter bearers carried several more severely wounded men into the hospital tent. He heard a doctor's surprised exclamation at a Choctaw Indian who had walked in with a little help. The man had seven bullet holes in him.

"Tough!" Ormond remarked.

St. Cyril hardly paused in his eating. "Didn't hit a vital spot."

Just then Colonel Roosevelt and three men rode into the clearing, trailing two pack mules. "Where's the commissary officer?" he demanded, breathlessly. His khaki uniform was sweat-stained.

"Right here, Colonel." A thick-set man stepped out into the sunlight. "What can I do for you?"

"Need as much food as we can pack on these animals,"

he said, dismounting. "My men have been stripped of everything."

"What?"

"Dammit, man, get a move on! I haven't got time to answer questions."

"I need authorization to. . . ."

"I outrank you, Captain. We'll worry about the paper-
work later. Show me where the stores are. We need to load
up and get back up that trail before sunset. Those Rough
Riders haven't had a bite to eat since morning."

"This way."

"My men stacked their packs when they went into the
fight. We returned later and found that those damned
Cuban *insurrectos* had cleaned us out. Stole our food, blankets, clothing . . . everything."

"The supplies are stacked over there, Colonel," the commissary officer said. "We're trying to get them under cover
before another rain."

"You, men, get these pack animals loaded up," Roosevelt said, striding away toward the mountain of boxes piled
near the pier. He began heaving cases of canned tomatoes
and beans off the stack. "Here, strap these to that pack
saddle. Get one of the mule packers to throw a diamond
hitch over the load so it won't shift or fall off."

"Colonel Roosevelt, those canned vegetables aren't for
distribution," the commissary officer said.

"Why not? Then I'll buy them with my own money."

"Sorry, sir. Regulations say these can only be purchased
for officers."

Roosevelt looked astonished. His face reddened. "Hang
the regulations! We're taking this food to some gallant
fighting men . . . officers and enlisted alike. If you want to
be a stickler about some silly regulations, you can prefer

charges against me through Colonel Wood."

"Hey, you!"

Ormond didn't respond until someone shoved his shoulder.

"I'm talking to you, mister!"

It was Private Rod Brumer, one of the men with Roosevelt. Brumer's sneering face with its bent nose was only three feet away when Ormond turned around.

"Yeah, I thought that was you!" Brumer said. "You ran all the way back here and you ain't even winded!" He laughed. "You left in such a hurry, you dropped your Krag," he continued. "Even has your initials, P O, scratched on the stock," he said, indicating the carbine hanging from a loop on his McClellan saddle. "Wasn't even fired."

"Brumer, get over here and help with this loading!" a corporal shouted.

"In a minute."

Ormond started to move off.

"Don't ignore me when I'm talking to you!" Brumer snapped. He took two lunging steps and yanked Ormond around to face him. "Look up yonder," he said, pointing toward the top of the jungle-covered ridge. Black vultures wheeled silently against the blue sky. "They're just waitin' their chance to pluck the eyes out of our boys lyin' dead up there . . . boys you might've helped save if you'd had the guts to fight."

Other men nearby were staring at this outburst.

Ormond felt himself flushing. He sized up his tormentor who was about his own height but more compact and muscular.

"I saw you run like the devil was blisterin' your tail. I hollered, but you was making tracks outta the line o' fire."

Ormond tried to keep his expression neutral. He knew his actions would eventually lead to something like this, but hadn't expected anything so virulent.

"You don't deserve to be up there with Ham Fish and the others who won't be going home. This is from them, you yellow bastard!" He spat on Ormond's shoes.

Something snapped in Ormond's head. His fist shot out and smacked the bent nose, spattering blood. Brumer staggered back. Ormond's fury loosed a flurry of blows before Brumer could recover. Several of his swings missed, but most connected solidly.

Brumer fought back, but Ormond was barely aware of the blows to his face and body. Frustration and pent-up anger drove him wildly into his opponent, and the two of them went down, rolling in the dirt.

Before either could gain an advantage, they were dragged apart by several strong men.

"If you two want to fight, there are plenty of Spaniards!" Roosevelt said, coming up to them. "Brumer, there's plenty of work to do. Hop to it! And you . . . ," he turned to Ormond. "What's your troop?"

"B Company, sir," Ormond replied through a rapidly swelling lip.

Roosevelt turned and grabbed the Krag off Brumer's saddle. "Here . . . take this and hie yourself back up that trail. Report to Captain McClintock. No . . . he was wounded. Find First Lieutenant Wilcox who's now commanding B Company. Tell him we'll be along directly."

"Yes, sir!" Ormond's arms were released, and he saluted, taking the carbine. He straightened his dirty, torn clothing and went to find St. Cyril.

"Good job!" the reporter said. "Saw the whole thing. I was hoping you'd knock his damned head off!"

Ormond touched the bruises on his cheek bone. "Self-defense . . . the only reason for fighting." He leaned to his left, favoring sore ribs. "The colonel ordered me back up there."

"I heard."

Ormond held up the Krag. "What are the chances I would even get my own carbine back? If this isn't a crazy world. . . . I guess I either go or get court-martialed for disobeying a direct order from a colonel." He snapped open the magazine on the side of the weapon. It was still fully loaded, as Brumer had said. He let out a long breath and snapped the loading box shut. "Maybe this was meant to be. . . ."

"Don't tell me you're beginning to believe in the inevitability of providence," St. Cyril said.

"I'm not sure what to believe any more."

St. Cyril eyed him critically. "I've known you only a few weeks. You have a lot of good qualities. But decisiveness is not one of them. Right or wrong, make up your mind what the hell you want to do, then do it. Stop trying to second-guess yourself, *reacting* instead of *acting*."

"You going to be all right if I leave you here?"

St. Cyril nodded. He handed Ormond the flask. "Finish this off, then move out and find Gunderson."

Ormond gulped the last two swallows of fiery brandy, and returned the flask.

"Keep your head down and your mouth shut. You'll get through this."

The can of stew and the brandy had fortified Ormond, along with a long drink of water from a canteen he'd appropriated. The fight had seemed to clear his head of uncertainties. He shifted the carbine to his right hand and started up the trail.

Chapter Fourteen

"B Troop, Atten . . . *shun!*"

Row on row of men snapped to—men who, a few minutes earlier, had been slouching, bare-headed, and singing "Rock of Ages", some with tears in their eyes, after Chaplain Brown had read the Episcopal burial service.

It was just after sunrise the next morning and they stood rigidly silent in ranks, unshaven faces shaded by shapeless campaign hats, salt-whitened blue shirts, baggy khaki pants secured at the calf by canvas leggings, their Krags' steel butt plates resting on the ground.

The bugler moistened his lips and brought up his horn. The mournful notes of "Taps" drifted out on the still morning air, calling the seven Rough Riders to their final rest.

The soldiers were in a clearing at the top of the trail, not far from the ambush site. Ormond and Gunderson had volunteered to help trench out a common grave in the hard soil with short-handled shovels. Pulling their polka dot neckerchiefs over nose and mouth against the stench of rapid decomposition, they grasped each blanket-wrapped corpse and placed it beside the others in the bottom of the four-foot-deep hole. Ormond shivered at the feel of the stiffened limbs and averted his gaze from a gashed and ghastly pale face when one of the blankets fell open. The land crabs and the vultures had been interrupted at their grisly meal when the bodies were collected.

Ormond had to remind himself that these were not men, but only the shells that had housed them. He was merely helping dispose of husks after the locusts had departed.

Other soldiers filled in the trench with loose, rocky soil and planted a row of upright headboards with each man's name, rank, and date of death.

As the last notes of "Taps" faded, Ormond reflected on these first combat fatalities—an Indian, a cowboy, a miner, a packer, a college athlete, a man from the Western plains, and a young man of the Eastern elite social register. To him, their deaths were only symbolic; their sacrifice had accomplished nothing. *I could have been in that grave myself.*

He thrust these thoughts firmly from his mind as the detail broke formation. No more morbid thoughts. He was determined to get a grip on himself, to take charge of his emotions. Even the fight with Brumer had been only an emotional reaction, not a controlled decision.

"Glad you and Roosevelt brought those supplies," Gunderson said as the two men tramped down the tall grass in the field and prepared to erect their dog tent in a row with others. "About all we had to eat yesterday was some beans we took from the pack of a dead Spanish mule. I was hungry enough to eat my leather carbine sling."

Ormond said little while the men set up camp in an open area atop the ridge. He was in a reflective mood, grateful Gunderson chose not to dwell on the panic flight.

When Ormond had made his confession, Gunderson had said: "I wondered where you'd gone. A couple of the boys mentioned later they saw you heading for the rear. Two others ran," he had related, matter-of-factly. "One of them was a lieutenant."

Ormond had glanced down, embarrassed to know he was among the cowards.

"Look, don't worry about it. I've seen men run from a stampede, from a stalking puma, from a saloon fight, even when they all had guns to defend themselves. It's a natural reaction. The main thing is . . . you're back. I was worried about you."

"What was the general feeling?" Ormond had inquired.

"Oh, I'd say the ones who even knew about it or mentioned it, sort of treated it as a sickness. Rather than being angry, they pitied you."

"Reckon they could tell by this fat lip and my bruised face that I'd been into it with someone."

"Everybody here looks rough for one reason or another." Gunderson had shrugged. "Here, stretch out that corner and peg it down," he had said, gripping a handful of the canvas shelter.

The Rough Riders bivouacked for the next two days, while the higher-ranking officers consolidated their position and brought up more troops. The Spaniards had retreated toward Santiago, which was now the next objective. Speculation ran through the camp that the entire war would be fought here on the south coast of Cuba. Any decisive battles would be nearby. Once victory was secured—and no one doubted that it would be—they'd carry out a triumphal celebration in the decadent capital of Havana, miles away where the Spanish authorities would formally capitulate.

The Rough Riders awaited further orders, enduring heavy tropical downpours every afternoon. The pack trains brought word from the coast that General Shafter was literally bending his buckboard with his 300-plus pounds to re-connoiter troop positions in relation to terrain. They were relieved to hear he was placing a priority on establishing his supply lines by mule over the muddy, slippery trails from Siboney. Even if this meant nothing better than sowbelly, hardtack, and coffee, at least there would be adequate supplies of that.

After the first clash at Las Guasimas, it took two days for the troops to talk out the details of their experience. Ormond kept to himself when not on sentry duty, or taking his turn pounding coffee beans and cooking. He responded to orders from the sergeant; otherwise, he spoke only to Gunderson. The men in his and adjacent companies had begun to grumble about inactivity. Most of them had survived unscathed, so far, and were eager for more action. Unconfirmed rumor had it that a large contingent of Spanish soldiers was advancing from the west to reinforce Santiago. And the semi-official word—supposedly secured from one of the majors—was that the Rough Riders and regular infantry would try to capture Santiago before additional Spaniards arrived.

"Santiago's only about five miles from here as the buzzard flies," Gunderson said. He and Ormond leaned on the lip of their trench and stared at the sunset. They were technically on sentry duty, standing ankle-deep in mud, their Krags at hand.

A green, basin-shaped valley stretched before them. Among the trees below, they could see glimpses of muddy water where two small rivers bisected the valley. The road from Siboney to Santiago, although invisible from where they stood, crossed this valley.

"There's San Juan Heights." Gunderson pointed at a sparsely treed ridge rising above the jungle at the far end of the valley. "The road crosses that ridge and drops into Santiago, a mile beyond."

"The advance looks simple enough from here." Ormond was studying the terrain through binoculars furnished that day to the sentries. "Except for that blockhouse with the red tile roof up top there."

"Supposedly crammed with Spaniards," Gunderson said, yawning. "Wish I had a cigarette." He seemed unconcerned.

Ormond slowly scanned the distant hills and valley. "There's a village two or three miles off, a little to the north."

"El Caney," Gunderson said. "That village is in the way of our march on Santiago. Heard Lieutenant Wilcox talking to Roosevelt. General Shafter and Wheeler and the rest of the high command seem to think we'll have to capture El Caney before we assault that ridge. That village and the blockhouse are apparently the only defense of Santiago."

"You sound confident."

"Might as well be."

"Never underestimate the enemy."

"Not likely. They've already burned us some. But, for all we know, the Spaniards over in that blockhouse are shaking in their boots. Judging from the way they ran, I'd say they're more afraid of us than we are of them."

"A strategic withdrawal to a stronger position," Ormond said, recalling the bullets zinging through the trees. For him, the Spanish had not fled soon enough.

"We'll deal with them," Gunderson said.

"From the looks of a couple captured guns, those Mausers are even better than our Krags."

"Depends on who's handling them," Gunderson said.

The sun dipped behind the distant hills, leaving the sky

a sheen of reddish gold. The faint, strange music of a Spanish bugle drifted across the valley.

Slowly the glow faded, and dusk wrapped them all in its dark cloak. For some inexplicable reason, Ormond thought of the stolen gold coins. Perhaps he would meet the Grim Reaper in the coming days and thus escape the consequences of being a thief.

"Shit!" he hissed aloud. He was falling back into his ingrained habit of thinking. Escaping, running—that's all he'd been doing most of his life. It was high time—as St. Cyril said—to act, not react. He would get through this damned war, go home, and then decide how to settle the debt he owed his father.

On June 30th orders came down for the regiment to move.

"About time!" Gunderson said, falling into line.

Ormond tried not to think ahead.

"Each man is to carry three days' rations and a full canteen," a sergeant said. "Everything else except arms and ammunition is to be left behind."

Because of fever and disabling wounds among the officers, there was a consequent shuffling of assignments, and Lieutenant Colonel Roosevelt became direct commander of the 1st Volunteer Cavalry regiment.

At noon the Rough Riders struck camp and drew up in column beside the road in the rear of the 3rd Cavalry. The road they were to travel—only a narrow, muddy track—was already choked with troops.

"Same old horse manure," Gunderson muttered as the Rough Riders, after standing in ranks for a half hour, sat down in place to wait while regiment after regiment passed. The sultry day wore on as he and Ormond watched the tangled mass of troops begin to unsnarl themselves and move forward at a turtle's pace.

Finally, toward mid-afternoon, the 3rd and the 10th Cavalry marched and the Rough Riders fell in behind them. But the massive column proceeded in fits and starts. Every few minutes they stopped, and Colonel Roosevelt, who was with them on horseback, ordered the men to lie down and loosen their packs. The heat and humidity bore down on them. No breeze penetrated the thick growth. Several of the soldiers seemed on the verge of heat stroke.

Now and then they emerged into an open space where some regiment was camped. Occasionally one of these regiments, which apparently had been left out of its proper place, would file into the road, breaking up their line of march.

Twice they had to ford small streams. Twilight came on, and then full darkness, but still they marched. About eight o'clock, the Rough Riders turned left and climbed a low hill at a place the officers called El Poso. On top sat a ruined ranch house. Colonel Wood conferred with Roosevelt on camping the brigade.

Roosevelt directed the Rough Riders to string out across the road into the jungle and each man was to pick a spot and lie down, sleeping on his arms. Sergeants posted the sentries.

Ormond, through sheer exhaustion, slept about four hours and, fortunately, there was no rain that night to disturb his sleep.

On July 1st, they all awoke before dawn. The men kindled fires, fried bacon, and soaked hardtack in the grease. The prospect of battle apparently did not affect Gunderson's appetite, but Ormond had to force himself to eat, knowing he would need the energy. Roosevelt even got his hands on a sack of beans and distributed them, enough for each man to have a small handful.

The sun rose about six, and the men fell in. Teams of horses hauled a battery of field guns up to the crest of the hill. The mountain howitzers were wheeled into position to begin firing toward San Juan Heights at the same time General Lawton's infantry began its assault on the village of El Caney, several miles to their right.

Ormond and Gunderson, standing at ease, were in position for a good view of the action. The first guns sounded from El Caney, and the howitzers opened up with a roar, belching white smoke. After each recoil, artillerymen rushed forward to roll the guns back into position, ejecting empty shell casings, and loading another round. Smoke obscured the top of the hill and drifted up to blot part of the clear blue sky. The acrid smell of burned powder assaulted Ormond's nose.

"Hold fire!" an officer cried.

The guns fell silent while two officers with binoculars scanned the distant target for results.

Less than a minute later something whistled overhead. A shell exploded. Shards of metal ripped through the vegetation. Another shell followed close behind and the aerial burst sprayed the hilltop with shrapnel. The two colonels leaped to their horses, shouting orders, even as a third shell burst among a group of Cuban insurgents, killing several.

The Rough Riders hardly needed an order to scramble off the hill. They scattered into thick underbrush below the crest. Colonel Wood's led horse was killed. Two or three regulars were wounded, one of them losing a leg to a great shell fragment.

"Helluva way to start the morning!" Gunderson said, as he floundered through the brush in response to Roosevelt's shout to form up by companies.

Ormond grunted a reply. He had withdrawn into himself, purposely blocking out sights, sounds, and activities around him, trying to insulate his mind against everything but immediate orders.

As soon as the firing ceased, Colonel Wood formed the brigade, with Roosevelt's Rough Rider regiment in front. In a column of fours they marched down the trail toward the ford of the San Juan River. Once again they marched, stopped, and marched again, passing two regiments of infantry. With each halt, Ormond concentrated on the natural world around him, ignoring the troopers choking the narrow trail. The sky was blue, small birds twittered, while brightly colored tropical birds filled the air with their squawking, as if to complain about the human turmoil around them. Ormond relaxed as much as possible, enjoying the cool shade where the trail was overhung with leafy branches.

The march resumed down the road that led between hilly ridges. Cactus and undergrowth closed in on either side, showing evidence of long-abandoned fields. Mists of early morning drifted upward and dissipated, the rising sun sucking up the moisture. The road gently curved and dipped and Ormond could see the column of blue-shirted men stretching far ahead.

A staff officer rode by, then a mounted orderly. The men crowded to one side in the narrow road to give a battery of field artillery room to pass.

From a distance came the boom of cannon.

At one halt they saw a large man on horseback in the shade of a trailside tree. Ormond recognized William Randolph Hearst. He looked as if he'd just stepped ashore from New York, dressed in a black suit, a jaunty, flat-brimmed straw hat with a scarlet hatband, and red tie to match. His private yacht lay just off Siboney, with a printing press aboard.

"Hey, Willie!" Soldiers up and down the ranks shouted a familiar, friendly greeting.

The publisher never moved or acknowledged the hails. He sat, pokerfaced, as if he thought the troops were jeering him. Ormond, for one, would have. He wondered if the famous publisher slept well at night, knowing he was in great part responsible for the carnage that was about to take place. Hearst had fanned the emotional flames for war through his New York *Journal*, with sensationalized half truths, rumors, and outright lies.

As if reading Ormond's thoughts, Gunderson jabbed a thumb toward Hearst and said, a little too loudly: "He's probably a good Christian who doesn't believe in drinking, gambling, or swearing."

"And he contributes to widows and orphans," Ormond said.

"Contributes to *making* widows, too," Gunderson added as they resumed the march.

"Hot, damn! Look at that!" A soldier was pointing upward.

A gas observation balloon with a wicker basket was bobbing above the trees behind them. Four members of the Signal Corps drew it along the trail with long tethers.

A Spanish shell whistled overhead and burst in a shower of deadly shrapnel.

"Damn' fools! Putting up that target for the Spanish artillery. They wouldn't know our position except for that yellow balloon!"

Besides artillery, enemy riflemen zeroed in on the jungle trail. Mauser bullets began zipping and whining overhead. The troops surged forward, pushing those in front a little faster. The road sloped downward toward the river, and Ormond slogged on, nearly oblivious to the fact that every minute or two a man near him would grunt and fall without a cry, shot through the heart or head. Ormond's mouth and throat were dry. In spite of the heat, he felt chilly surges in his stomach. He never paused to help drag the bodies of the dead or wounded out of the way of marching feet.

To the right of them, one of their field artillery pieces let go a terrific blast, stinging the ears. A huge cloud of white smoke erupted above the jungle, further advertising their position. Spanish gunners with smokeless powder quickly fixed their aim on this new target. Overhead, thin, seething sheets of bullets advertised the rapid fire of enemy machine-guns, firing blindly and high. The cracking of rifle fire was growing sharper.

The Rough Riders no longer marched together. Other units had crowded in and a mixture of volunteers and regulars now flowed along the trampled path. Ormond and Gunderson followed the example of several Rough Riders who'd turned aside from the trail to puncture cans of beef hash. Ormond had no saliva and had to choke down a little of the hash, with swallows from his canteen. The men stood sweating and eating in the breathless heat, no longer aware of the snippets of bullet-clipped leaves drifting down around them.

They fell into the line of march once more until the order was passed to drop their horse-collar blanket rolls. Relieved, Ormond shrugged out of his burden, feeling lighter and cooler.

Three civilians left the road and started down a side trail.

Ormond wiped sweat from his eyes. "Damnation! That's J. Stuart Blackton."

"Who?" Gunderson asked.

Ormond pointed at the man's two assistants who carried a black box about half the size of a steamer trunk. Stenciled on the side of the trunk were the words **Vitagraph Moving Picture Company**. "They're going to make a picture of a real battle."

"Good luck with that," Gunderson said.

In about one minute the three civilians came jogging back to the main trail, the black box showing two ragged shrapnel holes. The Spanish had zeroed in on the observation balloon and were making it too hot for any picture taking.

The Rough Riders continued down the shadowy trail, bent over to shield their bellies. Another overhead shell burst with a sound like a popping paper bag. The soldier next to Ormond caught a fragment of iron that shattered his shoulder blade. He slumped to the ground. Ormond stared.

"You OK?" He felt Gunderson's hand on his arm.

"Yeah."

Boom!

Shredded metal scythed through the human throng, leaving bloody heaps. But there was no panic. Men on the outer ring of the burst gave way, then closed up and went on. Motionless legs stuck out of the brush on either side of the trail. Ormond was numb to the havoc around him.

As the trail neared the water, the pack of soldiers grew denser. Men to either side of the narrow path threw themselves onto the matted vegetation to crush it down so others could pass. No orderlies could get through. A shouted order was passed from mouth to mouth to advance to the river and deploy.

"Deploy, my ass!" yelled a sergeant near Ormond, hacking at a tangle of vines with a Cuban machete. "Like trying to deploy a regiment through a pile of fishnets!"

Officers and sergeants were shouting for F Company, C Company, M Company to move forward. Volunteers and regulars were hopelessly mixed. There was no order to the units; the entire throng surged forward *en masse*.

Ormond managed to stick close to Gunderson, but they found themselves shoulder to shoulder with men from the 9th Infantry. Through the tunnel of their jungle trail, the ford was visible ahead. Ormond's foot slipped, and he looked down to see mud formed by the blood of the dead and wounded. He'd so insulated himself, blunting his emotions, that even this sight failed to move him.

Suddenly, as if a cork had popped out of a bottle, they were in the open, wading, thigh-deep, across the ford. Men pushed and ducked, running and splashing across the sixty-foot-wide stream. On the far side they scrambled out to take cover under the lip of a steep incline.

Ormond and Gunderson flopped down, panting, side-by-side, gripping their Krags, safe for the moment. Friendly and enemy fire cracked and boomed. Ormond could hear the steady drumming of their own Gatling guns that had gotten into action, returning fire toward the block-house on San Juan Heights.

"Bloody ford!" Gunderson said, glancing back at the carnage.

Chapter Fifteen

"Give me your canteen," Ormond said. He snatched the nearly empty container from Gunderson and, leaving his Krag, scrambled upstream in the shelter of the steep bank. He plunged into the cool water above the mass of fording men, pulled the corks, and thrust the two metal canteens under to let the cleaner water gurgle in. After corking, he stood in the stream and bent to take a good, long drink.

"Get out of there, soldier!" a lieutenant shouted at him. "No drinking. Get across!"

Ormond shouldered the canteen straps and waded toward the bank without answering the agitated officer. It was as if the lieutenant were shouting at someone else. Ormond felt the detachment of a spectator, not the emotions of a participant. He'd either succeeded in inuring himself to all feeling—fear, excitement, anger—or he was numb with shock.

Five minutes later, Roosevelt splashed his mount across the ford, trying to reorganize his Rough Riders into a unit and move them ahead.

The men rallied to his cries and orders. A few at a time, they scuttled, crawled, and dashed fifty yards farther into the partial shelter of a sunken road lined on each side by a barbed-wire fence.

There, men from the mixed companies of Rough Riders were pinned down by rifle and machine-gunfire coming from the old sugar mill atop Kettle Hill. The crashing of exploding artillery, the popping of rifle fire, and bullets whining off rocks, punctuated by the staccato rapping of machine-guns and Gatlings made conversation nearly impossible. Individual soldiers dared a few return shots above the embankments, but the hail of zipping, zinging bullets began taking their toll as first one, then another soldier jerked backward and slumped down, shot through the head or chest.

"Stretcher bearers!" The sergeant's shout was nearly drowned in the tumult.

Ormond kept his head down and let the roar of battle numb his senses. His mind wandered to the empty silence and fresh-smelling sage of the Arizona desert. The booms of artillery became thunder over desert mountains as he transported himself to the peace of another place, another time.

Captain Bucky O'Neill paced up and down near his Company A, the ever-present cigarette clutched between thumb and forefinger.

"Don't get rattled, men. They're just wasting ammunition." There was no excitement in his strong voice that rose above the din. "Take a deep breath and hold your fire. Be calm." The tall, lean company commander might have been on a social outing. "When they stop to take a breath, we'll be on 'em like a mountain lion on a lame deer."

"Cap'n, you'd best get your head down," a crouching sergeant advised.

"Hell, the Spanish bullet hasn't been made that can kill me," O'Neill replied. He turned away to say something to a lieutenant nearby. He started to speak, but his head jerked back as a bullet entered his mouth and exited the back of his neck in a fine spray of blood. He fell backward into the dirt without a sound.

"Captain! Captain O'Neill!" Three soldiers rushed to his side.

"Damn! They got him. Stretcher bearer!"

"No need to call for a litter," a lieutenant said, examining the fallen man. "Killed instantly."

"Those bastards will pay for this!"

More curses and exclamations were lost in the roar of gunfire.

Colonel Roosevelt yelled for an orderly. "Find General Wheeler. Tell him we're pinned down in an untenable position. I'm requesting permission to move forward."

The orderly saluted and leaped onto his plunging horse.

Minutes dragged by. Ormond pulled himself back to the present from his mental sojourn. He lay prone against the dirt bank and glanced at the position of the sun. It had hardly moved. Sweat dripped off his nose onto his carbine. He caught Gunderson's eye.

The grimy, unshaven man gave him a grin. "Helluva way to make a living!" he said.

The orderly galloped up and yanked his horse back on its haunches. He sprang off and said something to Roosevelt. A shell exploded on top of the cut bank, showering them with dirt. Everyone dived for cover.

Roosevelt jumped up. "Sergeant Wright!"

The six-foot, six-inch standard bearer rushed over to him.

"Break out the colors. We're moving on Kettle Hill!"

Wright slid the sheath of oilcloth off the furled banner.

"Rough Riders! On your feet! General Wheeler wants us to kick 'em in the teeth!"

A whoop came from the men nearest who could hear him.

A corporal jogged up, leading Roosevelt's horse, Little Texas, and the feisty lieutenant colonel swung into the saddle.

"CHARGE!"

Waving his pistol overhead, the mounted commander lunged out of the sunken road and galloped ahead. The men swarmed from their partial shelter and followed on foot, yelling, trailing the tall Sergeant Wright who waved the colors.

Ormond and Gunderson dashed, side-by-side, up the steep incline that was free of underbrush. The few scattered trees did not impede their view of the old mill above them. Ormond caught glimpses of straw hats and white-coated figures behind sand-bagged barricades. Gunfire from rifles and machine-guns blended into a roar.

Men stumbled and fell to the right and left and in front of him, but still the mass surged upward, throats roaring defiance. Men dropped to one knee, fired, jumped up, and went on. Roosevelt, conspicuous on horseback, seemed immune from harm. Ormond was caught up in a rush of fresh energy and fed off the strength of his comrades. He was once more a college football player rushing onto the field with his teammates, heedless, reckless, yelling at the top of his lungs, ready for physical conflict. There were no individuals here; they were one solid wall with one will—overrun the figures on top of the hill—or die.

A barbed-wire fence fifty yards from the top was flattened by the first wave, and the mass of blue-shirted men rolled on.

Ormond went to one knee, fired, and then, as he ran to catch up with Gunderson, worked the bolt. His lungs were heaving. He caught his foot on the flattened fence and went down, ripping his shirt sleeves on the barbed wire. A black soldier of the 10th darted past him.

The fortified mill came closer. Ormond jumped to his feet and ran forward, glimpsing grim faces, close muzzle flashes. Then the irresistible wave rolled over the parapet, sandbags toppling into the trenches behind. A few remaining Spaniards were shot at close range and several Rough Riders went down. Two or three pairs of combatants locked in deadly hand-to-hand struggles, rolling on the ground. The remaining Spaniards fled around the stone building and over the back side of the hill.

The winded soldiers fired several parting shots at the figures bounding wildly down the hill into the trees. But there was no pursuit. In less than a minute it was over, and the unfortunate white-clad soldiers who'd chosen to stand their ground lay dead. Bodies were strewn on the hillside and even more were sprawled in grotesque postures around the empty mill and its front barricade.

"Turn those machine-guns toward San Juan Heights!" Colonel Roosevelt yelled. "Make sure no Spaniards are skulking around inside."

"You hurt?" Ormond had Gunderson by the arm, but could say no more than two words at a time. His lungs were heaving.

The big man merely shook his head.

The Rough Riders and men of the 9th and 10th Infantry were swarming over Kettle Hill, searching the inside of the empty building, securing Mausers and bandoleers from enemy bodies.

Several yards from the ruined sugar mill an open-sided

shelter contained two large iron kettles that had given the hill its name. When interrupted by the charge, the Spaniards had been simmering a pot of beans with ham chunks over a nearby open fire.

Since all the Rough Riders' foodstuffs had been left behind with their haversacks and blanket rolls, Colonel Roosevelt put a sergeant in charge of ladling out as much hot beans as anyone wanted. Then he sent an orderly back to have supplies brought up by pack mule.

Ormond's carbine barrel was still too hot to touch and he leaned it against the wall on the porch. The weak, queasy reaction to this wild battle had begun to set in. But he had no time to think about it for an artillery shell burst overhead, spraying the hill with jagged shards of metal.

"Get under cover!"

"Train those machine-guns on San Juan Hill. Range . . . five hundred yards!" Roosevelt yelled, running toward the gunners who struggled to untangle the feeder belt and reset the water-jacketed guns on their tripods.

But the Spaniards, entrenched in the blockhouse on San Juan Hill, had the range. Their artillery shells continuously rained shrapnel down on the Americans, and the Spaniards supported this with accurate rifle fire.

Roosevelt was struck on the wrist by a small chunk of metal. It barely broke the skin, but raised a lump the size of a hickory nut. Two men at a time crouched behind the two iron kettles and fired at the enemy. Then deadly accurate Mauser fire killed four of them before an officer ordered everyone back into the building. Bullets clanged off the kettles.

One of the captured water-cooled Maxim machine-guns jammed, and the American gunners, unfamiliar with the weapon, were unable to get it working.

"Are they bringing up the Gatlings?" Roosevelt asked Colonel Wood who had joined him inside the main room of the mill.

"It'll be a while. Can't spare any horses to pull them right now. They can do just as well raking San Juan Hill from down there," he added.

Roosevelt looked aggrieved, but then brightened. "We turned the flank of San Juan Heights," he said, rubbing the knot on his wrist where the fragment of shrapnel had struck him.

Wood nodded. "A good thing, too . . . Lawton ran into a hornet's nest at El Caney. We've got Kettle Hill, all right, but those Spanish gunners over there have us in their sights."

"Will the infantry make a frontal assault on them?" Roosevelt asked.

"That was General Kent's intention, but I don't know when."

"With the fire that's concentrated on this hill, we can't wait here the rest of the day."

"I know," Wood said. "Keep the men under cover and get them something to eat for now. Have we got plenty of water?"

"No. That's a problem. That uphill charge in the heat took it out of the men. And the wounded are especially thirsty."

Another shell burst overhead, and both men flattened themselves against the wall as shrapnel shook dirt from the ceiling. The tile roof remained intact.

"Collect most of the canteens and send four men back down to the river to fill them," Wood said.

Ormond was eavesdropping on their conversation as he slurped hot beans from a dirty Spanish mess cup. He was surprised that he had an appetite.

"I'll go, Colonel," he heard himself saying. Hadn't Millard Johnson said never to volunteer?

"Good, Private . . . ?"

"Peter Ormond, sir."

Roosevelt corralled two other men who crouched at a nearby window, returning fire at the distant blockhouse.

The three began collecting empty canteens.

Ormond tossed aside his tin mess cup and ran outside where Gunderson squatted by the jammed machine-gun, trying to pry something loose.

"Here. We're going for water," Ormond said, swinging a shoulder full of empty canteens at him.

"We are?"

"Yeah. I volunteered you," Ormond said. He'd do anything to get off this hill. Again, he felt nauseated and wondered if he could keep down the beans he'd just eaten. Was it fear gripping his guts?

The four men jogged away from the mill.

Another shell burst overhead and Ormond felt a glancing blow to his head. Next thing he knew he was rolling over onto his back, tangled in the canteen straps. The tops of several palms tilted in his vision against the blue sky.

"Ormond! Where you hit?" Gunderson sounded far away.

He tried to respond, but couldn't make his mouth work. What had happened? At first the blow had not hurt, but now a fierce stinging burned his scalp. Warm blood trickled through his hair and into his ears. Gunderson and another soldier knelt beside him. One was wiping his face with a blue neckerchief. The other pressed a bandanna to his head. He knew he was hurt, but not how badly. At the moment, he didn't seem to care.

"Piece of shrapnel bit a hunk outta your scalp," Gunderson said. He turned to the other soldier. "I'll press this on it. You get a strip of cloth and bind it up tight. Scalp wounds can bleed like hell."

A few minutes later the dizziness passed and the tight bandage around his head slowed the bleeding. The pain was tolerable—only a dull ache. He struggled to his feet.

"Don't think an artery was cut," Gunderson said.

"Good. Let's go."

The other two men had gone on ahead and were out of sight.

"Probably oughta go upstream above the ford to get some cleaner water."

Gunderson nodded. "Probably just as dirty, but it looks cleaner. Fewer dead horses in it."

They angled across the hill and down into the trees that bordered the San Juan River.

"Here we go. This stretch hasn't been stirred up too much," Gunderson said. He slipped a dozen canteen straps off his shoulder and waded into the knee-deep stream. Bending over, he shoved the canteens under water. A rifle cracked and the big man went down, thrashing in the water.

Ormond saw a slight movement in a tree on the opposite bank. In one smooth motion, he drew the Bisley, swept back the hammer as he brought it up at arm's length and fired. He fired again before his pounding heart could jar his aim. A slim figure slithered out of the branches, caught on his safety rope, and hung upside down. His sniper's rifle clattered to the ground, twenty feet below. The dead man was camouflaged with small branches in his clothing.

Ormond's hands shook so much he couldn't hold his pistol steady. He swung around to be sure this was the only sniper in the area. Then he plunged into the stream where Gunderson was staggering up, trying to wade ashore.

"Caught a slug in the fleshy part of my calf." He plopped down on the bank.

A quick inspection showed the sniper's bullet had struck a glancing blow to the primer of a .30-40 Krag cartridge in one of Gunderson's belt loops as he was stooped over. The cartridge had discharged, his own bullet striking him in the leg.

"Bad luck," Ormond said, trying to keep his shaking voice steady.

"Good luck, you mean," Gunderson gritted, blood oozing between his fingers where he gripped his calf. "Couple inches the other way, and I'd have been gut shot by that sniper. You saved my life."

Ormond didn't want to take credit for his instinctive action. Hand/eye co-ordination was inborn. "He missed and I reacted."

"Damn' good shot with that Bisley."

Ormond looked at the sniper dangling by his belt from the tree. With the leafy branches covering much of it, the figure hardly appeared human. But it'd been a man only a few moments before—a deadly enemy who'd tried to shoot his friend from ambush. Would he react the same if he had it to do over? Yes. But he couldn't get rid of the ball of ice in the pit of his stomach. He'd ended the life of a fellow human—a life that could never be restored. He'd probably killed one or more he never saw in the heat of the charge. He'd have to think of that sniper as a criminal who needed to be executed. The killing was justified, but he'd taken a man's life. A silent voice deep inside told him something was wrong with this whole business.

With these thoughts whirling through his mind, Ormond

unlaced Gunderson's soaked legging and bound his own neckerchief around the wound. The bullet had exited a few inches above the ankle.

"Those small-caliber, high-velocity bullets make a clean hole." Gunderson's face was contorted with pain. "If that'd been a musket ball or a hunk of Civil War lead, it would've traveled slower and torn up a lot of tissue, even bone. I'd probably lose my leg."

Ormond was queasy and didn't want to talk about it. "Can you stand?"

"Think so. I might need a little support, though."

Ormond looked around. "Wonder what happened to those other two who came for water? Let's fill these canteens. If I can't carry 'em all, I'll make another trip."

Chapter Sixteen

An hour later, the Rough Riders, including some with minor wounds, were rested and refreshed with food and water. The one captured machine-gun that was still in operation was set up on the lip of a trench and trained on the blockhouse 500 yards away. The soldiers were running short of Krag ammunition. During the charge, several hundred .30-40 cartridges had been dropped as men tried to reload the loose ammunition on the run.

"That hillside is strewn with live rounds," Gunderson said. "Too bad we don't have time to make a search and pick them all up." He was seated at a window opening, taking careful shots at the tiny figures moving around the red-tiled blockhouse on San Juan Hill. His leg had been treated with alcohol and bound tightly with a clean bandage—taken from a medical chest hauled up with other supplies on mule back after the hill was secured.

"As long as we're wishing, I wish the Spanish would lay down their arms and go home," Ormond said, looking down on the advancing American forces near the base of San Juan Heights. From this distance, the infantrymen looked like tiny blue ants, swarming up the hillside. The soldiers were protected by the steep pitch of hill that hid them from entrenched riflemen on the crest. The Spanish gunners couldn't depress their cannon far enough to hit the American attackers.

"By Jove, Leonard, we've got them flanked!" Roosevelt said, lowering his binoculars. "Give me permission to attack!" He paced back and forth, glancing at Colonel Wood. "We can distract the Spanish while General Kent's infantry makes a frontal assault."

Another artillery shell whistled overhead and everyone dived for cover just before it exploded, spraying the area with shards of jagged metal. The two officers got to their feet, brushing off the dust.

"Leonard, my men are being picked off," Roosevelt said. "If we stay here much longer, morale is going to suffer. We're stationary targets. We must attack!"

Colonel Wood winced as a bullet chipped rock from the window sill and slammed into the opposite wall.

"Permission granted." Wood gave a tight smile. "Or, as our friend, General Wheeler, would say . . . 'kick 'em in the ass!' "

As if a tense spring had been released, Roosevelt sprang off the porch. "Come on, men!" His voice was raspy from yelling. "Charge!" He ran down the hill, waving his pistol.

In the roar of gunfire, Ormond didn't understand the command and wondered where his commanding officer was going. He looked after the running figure whose khaki pants were smudged with dirt and grass stain. White suspenders crossed over the back of Roosevelt's blue shirt that was dark with sweat. The loose ends of his blue and white polka dot neckerchief, tied around the crown of his hat, were flying out behind.

"Where's he going?" a soldier yelled into Ormond's ear

above the din as Roosevelt paused to kick down a tilted barbed-wire fence, jumped on a post to make sure it stayed flat, then continued running. Five men were jogging after him.

Fifty yards farther, he stopped and looked back. Just then a bullet cut down the man nearest him. Roosevelt ran back toward the sugar mill.

"Where are my men?" he yelled, red-faced and sweating.

The chatter of the Maxim machine-gun ceased.

"Are all of you cowards?" he shouted, his voice hardly louder than a raspy croak. "Come on! Charge!" He swung his arm toward San Juan Hill.

"Sorry, Colonel. We didn't hear you," Gunderson said, swinging the barrel of the machine-gun aside and grabbing his Krag.

A shout loosed the pent-up strain. It was taken up by others who scrambled to their feet, weapons in hand, and started after their stocky leader.

Ormond had put down his Krag inside the house while he helped feed the ammunition belt into the machine-gun. He had no time to find his carbine again, so drew the loaded Bisley from its holster and leaped up to join the rush. He knew if he stopped to think about this, the fear would be on him once more. Now it was only the adrenaline rush, the camaraderie, the wild excitement of the charge down the slope and up the long hill toward the pinnacle of San Juan Heights, 500 yards away.

The attack was a duplicate of the first, except the slope to the ridge was not as steep. But the fire from the trenches above was heavier than ever. Men were dropping on either side. He'd lost sight of Gunderson as the mass of Rough Riders and men from other units swarmed up the long, grassy hill. There were few trees to offer protection, but the men seemed heedless of danger. There was no order, no discipline. It was every man for himself and every man drew courage and strength from the massive wave of the charge. Singly soldiers dropped to one knee, fired, then jumped up and ran on, yelling. Men in blue jerked and tumbled as they caught the full force of the hot hail being driven down on them.

The drumming fire from friendly Gatling guns at the bottom of the hill kicked up puffs of dust along the ridge top. But, as the Americans neared the summit, the Gatlings ceased. Ormond felt invincible, oblivious to the men dropping all around. He was a king, a god, bent on wreaking vengeance on the dark-faced devils.

Suddenly the Spaniards were swarming out of the trenches and fleeing ahead of the assault. Ormond was carried over the sandbagged ditches in the first wave of Rough Riders, borne on a thunderous clamor of gunfire and shouts, his feet hardly touching the ground, unaware of pain or fatigue.

Roosevelt jumped onto the porch and fired a pistol at a white-clad Spaniard darting out of the blockhouse. The man dropped.

In the mass of bodies and confusion of heat, smoke, and blazing weapons, everything around Ormond seemed to slow down. He could see individual fights, men being shot from the side, from behind, two infantrymen attacking with fixed bayonets, a straw hat flying off, a spray of blood as a bullet exited the back of a man's head, could feel the breeze of a bullet fanning his cheek.

A Spanish soldier with a goatee worked the bolt of his Mauser and brought up the muzzle to point at Roosevelt's back several feet away. In Ormond's slowed perception, he had plenty of time to cock his Bisley, aim, and fire. The hammer fell on a spent cartridge. Instantly he flung the heavy pistol at the Spaniard. It struck him in the side of the head and he staggered, the Mauser jetting a tongue of flame into the wall. Before the man could regain his balance, Ormond slammed him to the porch floor, gripping the man's throat. The wiry Spaniard writhed with the strength of a giant python. He jerked up his knee into Ormond's groin. A sickening rush of pain caused Ormond to lose his grip. When he opened his eyes, the Spaniard was on top, reaching for a knife in his belt. Ormond grabbed the man's wrist and they struggled for possession of the blade, rolling over and over, off the porch, dirt flinging into Ormond's eyes.

Suddenly the ground went out from under them. Ormond landed on his back in the bottom of a trench, slamming the wind out of him. The Spaniard had his feet jammed on either side of Ormond, eyes gleaming with victory as he raised the big knife. The blade flashed down and Ormond twisted desperately to one side, feeling the sting of the razor edge graze his neck as the point buried itself in the ground. But the Spaniard fell forward, limply, on him. Ormond shoved him aside and Gunderson's sunburned face loomed above. The big man held the Krag he'd used to club the Spaniard. "Get your ass outta that hole!" he yelled. "We got 'em on the run!"

The Rough Riders secured the blockhouse atop San Juan Hill and began treating the wounded. Roosevelt had been ordered not to pursue the Spaniards toward Santiago, a mile farther to the west. It was an order Ormond, Gunderson, and the rest of the men received with relief. They'd had enough for one day and were physically and mentally exhausted.

When the rush of adrenaline ebbed, Ormond came crashing back to earth. His knees were so weak he sat on the edge of the porch for a half hour before he trusted himself to stand up and try to move around without vomiting. He found his nickel-plated Colt Bisley and reloaded it. He couldn't recall how many times he'd fired it during the battle, but vaguely remembered reloading it twice. Burned powder blackened the face of the cylinder and the muzzle. He shoved it back into its holster.

Ormond took no part in collecting the bodies that were strewn around, both American and Spanish. Many of the men were still euphoric, slapping each other on the back, yelling words of praise. There was no recounting individual exploits; that would come later. For now, they savored the victory.

Shortly a reporter appeared with his camera and set it up on a tripod to capture the historic moment for posterity. The Rough Riders, officers to the fore, grouped themselves for a photograph in front of the captured blockhouse.

"The glorious victory," Gunderson commented quietly to Ormond when the group broke up after the picture. "About sixteen dead and sixty wounded. And that's just among the Rough Riders," he added. "From the looks of things, there are a lot more dead infantry."

"Do you reckon *they're* feeling glorious?" Ormond wondered aloud. The cowardice and panic of a few days ago had been replaced by disgust. But now he understood mob mentality—by experience, if not by rationale. He had thrilled to the chase, the attack, the victory. Shooting Spaniards, he reflected, was caused by some frenzy, some unaccountable madness arising from his dark depths, which had suppressed his reason as surely as it had during his earlier fearful flight. He shook his head wearily. The complexities of his own humanity were more than he could fathom. To most men, war was a game, the overcoming of dreaded danger—a badge of manhood since the days when prehistoric hunters lived in caves.

Soldiers milled around, re-stacking sandbags by the trenches, salvaging a captured kettle of Spanish beans and rice, cleaning and bandaging their comrades' wounds. Roosevelt, Colonel Wood, and General Wheeler were in conference on the shady side of the blockhouse. A light westerly breeze flapped the Stars and Stripes that flew over the red-tiled roof. It was just past three o'clock.

Ormond leaned against a porch support in the shade. Gunderson sat nearby, running a cleaning rod through the barrel of his Krag, seemingly unconcerned with the distant popping of Spanish rifle fire.

For several minutes, both men remained silent. Finally Gunderson spoke to what was still on both their minds. "A lot of obscure things go to make up pride," he began slowly. "Yet courage, I believe, is nothing more than willful, stubborn pride. For whatever reasons, pride keeps a man from acting cowardly in the face of other men who are acting the same way for the same reasons." He chuckled. "Stupid, isn't it? None of us wants to lose face, so we'll all hoot and cheer and work ourselves up to the point where we'll murder our fellow man for vengeance, freedom, patriotism, self-defense . . . all kinds of excuses." With a final swipe of an oily rag, he began disassembling the cleaning rod for storage in the butt. "Yes, sir, the human animal is the most dangerous creature on earth."

But the fighting was not over. The rest of that day, Spanish rifle and artillery fire raked San Juan Hill, wounding several men. Roosevelt ordered able-bodied Rough Riders to work with shovels, lengthening and deepening the trenches. Others stacked sandbags. Some of the strongest and volunteers who couldn't sleep worked all night to accomplish as much as possible under cover of darkness. But Spanish sharpshooters kept firing at the grating sounds of shovels. Ormond worked for an hour before asking to be relieved and flopping down in a protected corner of the blockhouse to sleep.

The steady fire continued into the next day, with the Americans shooting back when they could distinguish a distant target. However, they couldn't spot the Spaniards who fired from the jungle with smokeless powder. The American gunners brought up two Gatling guns, removed the wheels, positioned them in the trenches, and aimed them at the blockhouses defending Santiago. Their intermittent drumming was a reassuring sound to Ormond's ears, even after the captured Maxim machine-guns had jammed. Four mountain howitzers were wheeled up by horses and added to the arsenal behind the sandbag parapet.

Gunderson complained that his stiffening leg made walking difficult. Ormond urged him to have a hospital volunteer clean the wound and change the dressing. One of the soldiers, treating the wounded in a field hospital below the lip of the ridge, hacked off a bamboo stalk and trimmed it with a machete to fashion a crutch for the big man.

Individual Spanish guerrilla fighters and snipers became such a danger, both from the front and rear of the entrenched troops, that Roosevelt sent a squad of men to hunt them down. These were outdoorsmen from Arizona Territory who were noted for tracking and marksmanship skills.

They returned that night and dropped six .45-caliber Remington rifles at Roosevelt's feet.

"We got eleven of them, Colonel," Private Goodwin said, as if he'd just shot his limit of ducks.

Ormond, who was standing nearby, could not help over-hearing men reporting to the commander just outside Roosevelt's tent.

"They won't be shootin' at stretcher-bearers, reporters, chaplains, and Red Cross men no more," Trooper Profitt added.

"I won't ask how you did it," Roosevelt said.

"Not as hard as stalking mountain lions or bears," Goodwin said. "We just spread out, and kept an eye open for a likely looking tree. Then one of us would show himself just enough to draw attention. If a sniper was hid up there, he generally had to move a tad to get a shot. If there weren't no wind, the other man would see the movement and bag him."

Soldiers manned the trenches in rotating shifts, those on night duty sleeping in the muddy bottoms with their weapons, leaving every fourth man as a guard.

"*Whew!* This is worse than actual fighting," Gunderson said two days later.

"I know," Ormond replied. "I feel the same way. Probably a mental letdown."

"Mine's physical. I'd like to test my theory by clamping my molars into a rare steak with all the trimmin's." Gunderson grinned through his scruffy beard.

The long-range sniping and artillery fire continued for three days. Finally General Shafter sent an aide, under a flag of truce, to General Toral, the Spanish commander, demanding the surrender of Santiago. Toral replied that he felt under no pressure to surrender, stating that all he had to do was wait a short time while jungle fever decimated the American forces.

General Shafter responded that 50,000 healthy replacement troops were on their way to Cuba. The basic points of these negotiations filtered to the Rough Riders in the trenches.

During the lull in the fighting, Roosevelt used his authority to confiscate captured horses and mules that weren't being used. Chaplain Brown, who had a knack for appropriating stray animals, assisted the colonel. The pair formed a pack train and made several trips to Siboney for supplies. Since the hill had been overrun three days earlier, men and officers had had nothing to eat but hardtack soaked in water.

The day after the truce began, Ormond was celebrating Independence Day by stabbing tomatoes out of a tin can with his knife blade. His body seemed to crave the tart acidity of the vegetable. He finished and tipped up the can to drain the juice when he saw a black face smiling at him.

"Millard Johnson! By God, it's good to see you!" He tossed the can aside and embraced his old friend. "Where you been all this time?" he asked, stepping back to arm's length. "By God, you look fit!"

"I 'spect I been eatin' a lot better than you." Johnson studied him a moment. "You sorta favor a scarecrow. Where's your friend, Gunderson?"

"Over there in the shade . . . probably wishing he had a drink to kill the pain of that leg wound."

"What happened to your head?"

"Caught a piece o' shrapnel a few days ago. Nothing serious. I get the bandage changed every day to keep it clean till it gets a good start healing."

Johnson nodded solemnly, looking around at the soldiers manning the trenches. "I see you got some colored troops here."

"Yeah. Soldiers of the Ninth and Tenth."

"Smoked Yankees."

"Huh?"

He grinned widely. "That's what those Spanish prisoners down on the coast been calling us coloreds."

"Talking about anything smoked makes me think of smoked herring, smoked ham, smoked oysters . . . anything to eat. We're starving up here."

"I been down at Siboney, cookin' fo' the officers . . . and the sick men in the hospital tent who can eat."

"Wish you'd brought up that Buzzacot oven," Ormond said, licking his lips. "Until today we been on hardtack and water since we took this hill. A few of the hunters foraged out in the jungle and shot half a dozen guinea hens, but they were all used for the sick."

"That's one reason I come up here . . . to cook up some o' that grub we brung up on the mules. Even got a fresh beef carcass one of the officers shot near Santiago. Reckon I better get to fixin' it before it goes bad in this heat."

"I'll get Gunderson. We'll be first in line."

For the next several days, the men ate beef, bacon, hardtack, potatoes, rice, cornbread, oatmeal, washed down with sweetened coffee.

"By God, this is heaven!" Gunderson sighed. He held up one of a dozen doughnuts Johnson had made as a special treat for him and Ormond. They quietly shared them with a few friends.

Four days later Johnson had to return to Siboney. Another pack train brought up more supplies. The mules could carry only enough for about a forty-eight-hour supply.

During the truce, various military attachés, foreign officers, and civilian newspapermen visited the camp below the crest of San Juan Heights. Ormond watched from a distance as they conferred with Roosevelt and other officers. To his delight, Dismas St. Cyril was among the correspondents.

"You must be feeling a lot better if you walked all the way up here." Ormond grabbed his friend by the shoulders.

"Decent food and a little rest will work wonders on a man's constitution and his outlook on life," St. Cyril said. "I even managed to get a little quinine for my malaria."

On July 9th, word filtered among the troops that General Shafter and General Toral had reach an agreement. To save face, the Spanish general would surrender with dignity while Santiago was under fire. Thus, the two commanders scheduled a mock bombardment for the next day. The Rough Riders were ordered into the trenches, or into the blockhouse, and told to stay under cover while this formality was carried out.

Gunderson, Ormond, and St. Cyril joined the general migration to the trenches at dawn on July 10th to watch the fireworks.

The range was an easy 2,000 to 3,000 yards to the flags fluttering over the Spanish fortifications. Captain Capron's battery began a very slow firing of the howitzers. *Boom!* White smoke billowed, and a shell burst over the jungle wide of its mark. He paced to the next gun, said something to the gunners, and moved on. *Boom!* The gun recoiled, lunging back on its scotched wheels. The shell exploded in the tree tops, far short of the Spanish trenches.

Captain Capron, a large, fleshy man, had taken to drinking heavily during his off-duty hours after his son, Allyn, was killed at Las Guasimas. Ormond noted the man's flushed face and bloodshot eyes that testified to another late night with the bottle. But Capron carried out his part in this farce as if it were the real thing. He stepped up to the next gun. "Number Three . . . fire!"

The cannon bellowed. A few red tiles flew into the air, along with a cloud of adobe dust from an already ruined building. With every miss, Captain Capron cursed and stormed up and down, grumbling to himself, in case any reporters were not in on the ruse. The men in the trenches grinned at each other, enjoying this charade.

"This is the way all wars should be fought!" St. Cyril remarked to Ormond. "Then, the two commanders could arm wrestle to decide a winner, and everyone would go home."

On July 17th, General Toral formally surrendered. The 9th Infantry marched into Santiago. Lusty cheers ran along San Juan Heights and the men waved their hats and guns in the air at the sight of the American flag being raised over the city.

The war was over. Ormond expected the Rough Riders to march down to Santiago, board a ship, and return home.

"In the military, nothing's that simple," Gunderson said the next day when he and Ormond joined their company in marching off San Juan Heights. They, along with a few units of regulars, had been ordered to bivouac in a large, grassy field west of the village of El Caney.

"Thought maybe we would celebrate in Havana," a nearby soldier said.

"Then you better have your marching shoes laced up," Color Sergeant Wright remarked, " 'cause Havana's about four hundred miles northwest of here."

"I reckon our ships have Havana harbor blockaded," another man added, "or surely the Spaniards would put up a fight to hold the capital city."

"Hell with it. Let the politicians fight it out now. We've done our share."

Conversations dwindled as the men began to breathe heavier, and the sun climbed higher, bearing down on backs bobbing under faded blue shirts. Forty men, weakened by fever, staggered and fell out of ranks during the two-mile march to the new campground. The men tramped down the tall grass in the big field and pitched their white dog tents in rows. Some of the strongest even salvaged boards from a nearby ruined building and fashioned floors for their tents, cutting bunches of long grass to pad them.

During the next two weeks, daily rains, steamy heat, mud, the lack of proper food or sanitation, wore down their natural resistance. One and two at a time they began to succumb. The Rough Riders lost more men to malaria, yellow fever, typhoid, and dysentery than they had lost during combat.

Ormond discovered there were three kinds of body lice. He considered himself fortunate to have only the kind that attached themselves to the hairs of the head. "Rough Riders," he said, digging at his itchy scalp with his fingernails. Several of the men laughed, and the lice got a new nickname.

From among the military supplies that now came by mule train from the closer town of Santiago, each man drew a cube of yellow soap. At the first opportunity, Ormond, Gunderson, and several others hiked down to the San Juan River to bathe. They discovered that the lice appeared to thrive on this yellow soap. There was not enough soap to wash their grimy pants and shirts.

They walked back to camp naked, carrying their vermin-ridden clothes over one arm.

"What do we do with these?" one of the men asked.

"Gotta wear 'em. We ain't got any others."

"I hear tell ants are vicious critters. They resent any intrusion into their territory," Gunderson remarked. "Why don't we spread our clothes out on those ant hills and let 'em do the dirty work of getting rid of the lice?"

This suggestion was met with general approval, so the rest of the afternoon two dozen men lounged around naked in the sun, watching their particular ant colonies in hopeful suspense.

By sunset, the net result of this experiment was two dozen sunburned men.

"The lice and the ants must've signed a peace treaty," Gunderson remarked, crawling into his dog tent after supper.

"I guess they aren't natural enemies, after all," Ormond said, wrapping himself in his blanket and shivering with a violent chill.

The troop ship captains motored their transports from Siboney and tied up at the Santiago docks. There, the able-bodied of the 71st New York Volunteers jacked the remaining supplies ashore, emptying the sweltering holds of half-rotten turnips, onions, and potatoes. The pack trains carried the sprouting, malodorous piles of vegetables to the soldiers still guarding San Juan Heights and to the Rough Riders in their new camp.

The standard canned beef, hardtack, and coffee were supplemented by piles of vegetable muck. "We've come a long way since we enlisted," Ormond said, trimming off a few good pieces of onion and potato to drop into their stew pot.

Gunderson looked up from crushing green coffee beans in the frying pan with the butt of his Colt. "At home, we'd be accused of eating out of garbage cans."

"I'll look with a lot more favor on the next bum I see in Saint Louis," Ormond said. "Want a shot of this?" He held up a bottle of Worcestershire sauce.

Gunderson shook his head. "Where'd you get that?"

"Digging through one of those mule packs. All kinds of

supplies showing up now." He took a swallow of the condiment. "It's good. Has a salty taste, and warms up the guts when you have chills."

The days dragged by and flecks of blood began showing up in the shallow latrine trench as dysentery took hold. Weakened men lay down beside the packed trail to the latrine. Ormond was returning from one of his frequent visits to the trench when he saw a lieutenant lying in the sun beside the path. He reached to help him up, but the officer waved him off. "I'll get there after I rest a little." Farther along, Ormond saw two more soldiers on the ground, garnering strength for the short hike to the latrine.

Ormond stopped when he saw Gunderson approaching from the opposite direction. A soldier passed them, bent over, holding his stomach. "We need some morphine to stop this dysentery," Ormond said.

"That'd clamp the bowels shut for sure. But Doc says the morphine's about gone. They're using what's left to ease the pain of the seriously wounded."

Ormond pushed up his hat. The breathless heat was stifling and he brushed away the buzzing flies.

"The government was all rarin' to go to war, but they forgot to get ready," Gunderson continued. "No organization, no decent food, almost no medicine."

General Shafter ordered all the water used for drinking and cooking boiled. A good idea, the men agreed, but pots for holding water were lacking. They had only their tin mess cups. At the San Juan River, water details met at the only nearby place where the banks were not as steep as the side of a house or matted with jungle. Here men bathed, with or without soap, and used the banks as a latrine. Mules came there to water. The placid little river flowed to other pools where other water details gathered, and down to Bloody

Ford where more canteens were filled daily.

Sickness and death raged on. More and more men reported to sick call each day. If a man had the strength to crawl out of his dog tent and report to sick call, he was considered fit for duty. Most men stayed where they were and took their chances, trying to make do. The doctors had only a few doses of quinine and morphine and little else but sympathy. So, being sent to the regimental hospital amidst even more filth and possible contagion was tantamount to a death sentence.

Each passing day, Ormond lay in his tent for hours, listening to frequent volleys of rifle fire, followed by "Taps". Finally these sounds ceased on order of the high command who were afraid the frequent funerals would hurt morale. But the blanket-covered litters continued to be carried out in a steady stream. Gravediggers and the chaplain were kept busier than ever.

At the end of July, General Shafter called all his officers together to discuss the situation. Their decision was unanimous. They all signed a letter requesting that Secretary of War Alger withdraw the 5th Corps from Cuba.

On August 7th, the Rough Riders, who could still walk, marched down to Santiago and boarded the transport ship, *Miami*, bound for Long Island, New York. Smelling of wood smoke, sowbelly, and rancid onions, Ormond and Gunderson supported each other and wobbled up the gangway, assisted in the crowd and confusion by Millard Johnson, who had slipped away from his duties as cook and mingled with the Rough Riders.

"By God, we escaped the hospital tent and the hospital ship!" Gunderson was panting from the slight exertion.

"So far, so good." Ormond looked at his two friends.

Gunderson leaned on his Krag like a cane. His strength

appeared gone and he sagged to the deck against a bulwark. He was lean and leathery, and a dark, ragged beard covered his lower face. His eyes were bright and glassy with malnutrition and fever.

Johnson, smiling under his Cuban straw hat, was the only one in the throng who appeared halfway healthy.

"I be seein' if I can get some food from the crew for you two," Johnson said.

Ormond glanced down at his own greasy pants with holes in the knees. His shirt had been torn by thorns and barbed wire.

"You still got those gold coins?" Ormond whispered. The two men moved aside from the gangway to make room for the press of soldiers behind them.

"Sho' do." He patted the stained leather belt. "Right here."

Ormond smiled weakly. "We're going home."

Chapter Seventeen

Ormond opened his eyes a slit and blinked. It took him several seconds to remember where he was. Then he heard a cough and murmuring voices, smelled camphor and urine. He was still in the hospital ward at Jefferson Barracks, Missouri.

But, for once, he felt rested. His heart rate had returned to normal and he was no longer feverish. He stretched out on his back under the sheet and stared at the high ceiling, feeling good. He'd slept the entire night without waking or needing a nurse to fuss over him. The fever had left him weak, but his hunger returned with a vengeance. Yesterday, he'd even felt well enough to allow himself to be shaved and have his hair trimmed. Four beds to his right, a nurse in a crisp white cap was changing the dressing on a soldier's leg.

It had been a long road from Cuba to this old military post just south of St. Louis. He could recall only segments of the journey; most of it had been suppressed by his feverish brain and periods of unconsciousness. The last few weeks came back to him as a series of scenes, like photographs, frozen in time—Gunderson and Johnson supporting him as he pretended to walk aboard the ship leaving Santiago; searing sun on deck; blue water and white clouds; the taste of salt in the back of his throat; landing at Montauk Point, Long Island; the chill of late summer rain on his overheated skin.

He recalled lying in a tent city of wounded and sick men. Disjointed memories consisted of bad food and water, the stench of dysentery all around him, no appetite, growing weaker, long periods of neglect, men cleaning the grass of blood and feces and disposing of the wooden crate latrines to prepare for a visit by the Surgeon General. There had been talk of a scandal because of how the sick were being neglected in Camp Wikoff. Visits by civilians and dignitaries were restricted to that section of the Long Island encampment that was not quarantined. The high command gradually loosened their strict control of Camp Wikoff to allow some healthy soldiers passes to New York City.

Ormond had rallied from his fevered malnutrition. Full of the wine of life, and the strength of false energy, he'd slipped out of the loosely guarded quarantined section to join Gunderson and Johnson. He remembered pleading with Gunderson: "If I'm going to die, I want to be closer to home."

Dismas St. Cyril had come ashore from the same ship and was writing an exposé of conditions at the hospital camp—the quarantined area attended by only one untrained and overworked orderly. St. Cyril had offered to suppress this stinging article if a medical officer would write orders transferring Peter Ormond to the military hospital at far-off Jefferson Barracks near St. Louis. As part of the deal, Privates Gunderson and Johnson were to escort him. The medical officer fumed at the coercion, but finally agreed.

The trip had been a nightmare of jumbled scenes—bright lights, days and nights running together, the overcrowded Long Island Railroad where he had slept on the floor of the passenger coach. He'd had a stretch of lucidity when they transferred to a train for Illinois. At Chicago, St. Cyril had left them. Another long ride had taken them southwest. There had been times when he had felt on top of the world, hungrily devouring bananas and milk and ham sandwiches at lunch counters in depots, his belly distended from malnutrition to the point where he could hardly buckle his belt.

He'd collapsed when they detrained in St. Louis, his heady wine of life drained. He had a vague recollection of being carried by litter and hauled off in a Red Cross ambulance to this hospital where he'd spent the last several weeks.

All that was behind him now. He sat up on the edge of the bed with a smile of satisfaction. He finally felt he was going to make it. Gunderson and Johnson had been discharged from active duty here a month before, but both were still in St. Louis, stretching out their Army pay, waiting for him to recover. They visited often, checking on his progress, cheering him. Gunderson talked of rounding up wild horses in Arizona for breeding. He wanted to go into business selling remounts to the cavalry and horses to ranchers. Johnson was keeping his options open but had offered to work as cook and handyman on Gunderson's new ranch.

At that moment, another visitor who'd been frequenting this long ward during the past week walked in the door. Ormond's heart beat a little faster at seeing an attractive volunteer he'd come to know as Mary McCarthy. The young woman came to visit the sick and wounded nearly every day, bringing them small treats of tobacco or candy, but mostly cheering them with her presence, letting them know someone cared. As far as Ormond knew, she had no connection with the Red Cross, the medical staff, or the military. She was just one of several women who made it their business to help.

She paused and exchanged pleasantries with a soldier sitting in bed with his head and arm swathed in bandages. Her laughter rippled softly along the ward like distant piano music. Ormond got up quickly and grabbed his clothes that hung near the head of his bed. He pulled on his dark blue uniform shirt and canvas pants that had been washed and sewn. The shoes were scuffed, but clean. His campaign hat, still hanging on the peg, was stained and shapeless.

" 'Morning, Peter." She stopped at the foot of his iron bedstead. "You look a lot better than you did just a few days ago."

"Hi, Mary." He was self-consciously buttoning his shirt. "I sure *feel* a lot better."

"Good." She eyed him critically.

"You bring a lot of sunshine into this place." He was surprised at his own words.

"Thanks," she said, graciously accepting the compliment. "Speaking of sunshine, it's a beautiful Indian Summer day. If you're up to a little ride in the fresh air, I've got my buggy outside."

"Can't think of anything I'd rather do." He glanced at the late September sun flooding through the row of open windows.

He signed out with the nurse on duty. Walking still tired him, but he didn't have far to go before climbing up into the open buggy. Mary sat beside him and took up the reins. She clucked to the sleek Morgan and moved out at a walk. When they rolled away from the three-story brick and stone hospital, Ormond looked back at the building that had been his home for more than a month. Several patients lounged on the upper verandahs. A splash of red and gold tinged the maples, and a warm breeze scattered some fallen leaves across the road in front of them.

"A day like this makes me glad to be alive," she said. "I even brought a picnic lunch." She nodded at a wicker basket under the seat.

"Uh . . . fine." Hungry as he was, he felt a bit uncomfortable, not being used to virtual strangers doing him special favors. Yet, if this beautiful woman were somehow attracted to him, that was a different story. He'd like to get to know her better. He surreptitiously pulled out a pocket comb and ran it through his thick hair.

She turned the horse off the road onto a grassy bluff overlooking the Mississippi River. They stepped down, and she tied the reins to a bush in the shade of a large elm. Ormond retrieved the picnic basket as she spread a blanket on a sunny, level spot.

"Hope you like fried chicken and potato salad."

"I love it. Sure beats the milk and egg white they've been feeding me."

"What?" She sat on the blanket, tucking her legs under the long, tan skirt.

"Truth. But I graduated to custard a few days ago. I'm dying for some real food . . . if my stomach will tolerate it."

"What exactly was the matter with you, anyway?"

He automatically put a hand to his healed scalp wound, but decided not to mention that. "Well, even the doctors aren't sure. All sorts of tropical disease experts poked and prodded me. When I first arrived, they even soaked me in ice water. I fooled them and survived their treatment." He chuckled. "But it did bring down my fever for a time."

She handed him a blue-checked napkin, then dished up

the potato salad on two tin plates while he selected a golden brown drumstick.

"They finally concluded I had something they called . . . Compound-Enteric-Typhoid-Malaria."

"Sounds impressive." She smiled.

"Well, bad food, bad water, Spanish bullets, and the jungle didn't kill me, so maybe I'll make it yet."

She poured the lemonade and they fell silent for several minutes while they ate.

"Delicious," he said between bites. "I'd forgotten how tasty real home cooking can be."

She smiled her delight at him. "What are your plans when you get out of here?"

"I've had a lot of time to think about that, and I've decided to partner up with a friend of mine, rounding up wild mustangs in Arizona and breeding horses for sale."

"Sounds exciting."

A light breeze wafted up from the river far below. The Mississippi was low and a long sandbar was exposed along the Illinois shore.

He finally put down a cleaned chicken bone, wiped his mouth with the napkin, and drew a long breath. "It doesn't get any better than this."

"Oh, yes, it does."

He looked his question at her.

"Did you wonder at all why I asked you out here?"

He nodded. "A little. Couldn't imagine it was 'because of my looks and killin' ways,' as the Irish say."

"Although you *are* handsome, and seem very nice, it was more than that."

He held his curiosity in check, staring at her. She wore a long sleeve, white shirtwaist, open at the throat to reveal a cameo brooch on a slender gold chain. Shoulder-length black hair was held back by a blue ribbon and the healthy glow of her complexion was like something right out of the mists of Ireland.

"I have something else for you." She reached into a deep pocket in the folds of her skirt and withdrew a slim, flat parcel, wrapped in soft chamois leather. She held it out to him.

Wondering, he took it. When he flipped back the wrapping, his heart gave a leap. It was his father's gold coins! He could hardly catch his breath as he looked at her. What he saw was the girl on the train. Her black hair was shorter, but now he began to recognize the features he had seen only briefly in a dimly lighted coach. She had remained in his mind these six months as a willowy, dark-haired young woman with striking good looks. But he had been unable to recall the details of her face—until now. It *was* the same girl. No longer was this woman before him the kindly hospital visitor, Mary McCarthy—she had taken on the uglier aspect of the ruthless pickpocket he'd come to hate. He tried to speak, but no words would come. He was completely dumbfounded.

"You look awfully pale," she finally said. "Are you all right?"

"You . . . ," he finally began.

"Yes."

"Why . . . ? How . . . ?"

He stared at the coins, then ran his hands over the flat wooden strips and touched the surfaces of the coins with his fingertips—the imprint of Pike's Peak on the Clark, Gruber & Company $20 piece, the raised image of the beaver on the Oregon coins. He had to assure himself he wasn't just delirious. Had she chopped up some hallucinatory mushrooms in the potato salad? Was this whole scene a fevered dream?

"Here. Take a swallow of this before you faint." She handed him a tiny, metal flask. He numbly took it and swallowed a dram of fiery liqueur that instantly cleared his head.

"OK, here's the story." The smile vanished from her face. "First of all, my name is not Mary McCarthy. Yes, I stole these while you slept on the train that night. The old man with me was my uncle, a snake-oil drummer down on his luck. He spotted you flashing those coins and insisted I get them. We were on our way to Kansas City to work a convention, but not in the normal way. You see, I'm a jewel thief . . . a very accomplished one, I might add. I stepped out of my usual line of work when I picked your pocket. As an Irish girl from a poor family, I long ago created a phony background of wealth and position for myself in order to blend in with society matrons. These are women whose inheritance, or husbands, or lovers afford them the finest of jewelry. How do I justify such high-class thievery?" She laughed with her mouth, but not her eyes. "Those who own such expensive baubles suffer from excess. Besides, their trinkets are insured and replaceable. I'm only redistributing some of this hoarded wealth. I'm skilled at my profession. Being a woman helps. They never suspect me."

"Why did you return these?" Ormond was beginning to realize this was actually happening.

"Simple. I couldn't sell them. Your father put out the word all over the country that they'd been stolen from him. He offered a sizeable reward. Every pawn shop owner, every coin dealer, every collector knew about it. I almost got caught several times trying to peddle them. It was like trying to fence the *Mona Lisa*. These coins are so rare they're instantly recognized by anyone with the money or interest in purchasing them. At least gems can be taken out of their settings, re-cut or altered so they can't be traced, and are easy to sell. Not so, with coins. I'm out of my field with coins."

Ormond nodded. "Why didn't you just return them for the reward?"

"I would've had to invent some story about how I got them. Your father's too smart and too powerful to swallow some cock-and-bull story. He'd have had me arrested. At the very least, my name and picture would have been in the papers. My anonymity would have been lost."

"You could have just dumped them into the river," he said, staring down at the Mississippi below the bluff.

"I'm a lover of beautiful objects . . . probably my only weakness. These coins are both beautiful and unique, and I couldn't bear the thought of them being lost forever. It is poetic justice that they come full circle and be returned to where I got them." She gave a wry smile. "Who knows? Maybe I even have a touch of patriotism in time of war."

"What? How did you find me?" Ormond could feel the blood returning to his face as the shock wore off.

She reached into the pocket of her voluminous skirt and pulled out a flat, leather purse. From it she extracted a folded newspaper clipping and handed it to him. It was from the Chicago *Evening Journal*. He was shocked to see a clear photograph of himself at the head of the column. "*Ahh*, Dismas Saint Cyril," he said, glancing at the by-line. "I'd almost forgotten about this." The photo and the interview had been St. Cyril's price for forcing the release of Ormond, Gunderson, and Johnson from the pestilent Camp Wikoff on Long Island. There was a cost to everything.

He swept his eyes down the lengthy article, picking out bits and pieces of his own story. It was almost like reading about some stranger. St. Cyril had neglected to mention his cowardice, but quoted Gunderson's account of the attack on San Juan Hill when Ormond had saved Theodore Roosevelt from being shot in the back. "Judging from this, you'd think I was some kind of hero." He handed the article back. "Most newspaper articles are a lot of fluff and exaggeration."

"I wasn't sure from the picture that this was actually you, but then I read your statement that you'd enlisted after you were robbed while riding a train. Then I *knew*. It winds up by saying you were recovering in the Jefferson Barracks hospital near Saint Louis, so I had no trouble locating you." She tucked the article away in her purse and returned it to her pocket. "Have you been in touch with your parents since you stole those coins?"

"No. Unless Saint Cyril's column is syndicated and that piece also appeared in a Saint Louis paper, they don't even know I went to Cuba, or that I'm here."

"Then you're probably unaware your mother had those coins fully insured."

"What?"

She nodded. "Only last week there was a spread on the society page of the Saint Louis *Post-Dispatch* about a lavish party she hosted to celebrate the settling of the insurance claim for her husband's collection. I guess the company required a waiting period of several months to see if the stolen gold would turn up."

"I was told by Millard . . . uh . . . by someone, that there was no insurance," Ormond said, trying to adjust his thinking.

She shrugged. "Evidently there was."

A wave of relief flooded over him. He'd bet anything his mother had quietly restored the policy on her own. She'd always been more practical than the old man. But it must have been difficult to find enough to pay the premiums, un-less she had some of her own inheritance squirreled away, or had sold some of her silver service.

"What do you want in return for the coins?" he asked.

"Nothing. I just want to be rid of the accursed things. They're worse than owning the Hope diamond. I've had nothing but trouble since I lifted them from your pocket." She rose and began cleaning up the picnic dishes. "If you want to consider me altruistic," she added, "then let's just say I'm doing my bit for our wounded soldiers."

Ormond, his head in a whirl, automatically helped.

When the basket was again stowed under the seat, she turned to him. "You'd best keep a grip on those coins in the future," she said, untying the reins of the Morgan.

"I'll return them to the old man," he said.

"You'll forgive me if I let you walk back to the hospital," she said, lifting her skirt to climb into the buggy. "In case you get any ideas about turning me in, I want time to be safely off this post and gone. No . . . stand back over there." She waved him away. "I have a loaded Derringer in my pocket."

"I wouldn't turn you in," he said. "In fact, I'd like to see you again."

"It would never work." She smiled. "But, thanks."

She turned the Morgan's head and snapped the reins over his back. The horse trotted up onto the road, pulling the rubber-tired buggy. The sound of clopping hoofs faded around a curve toward the main gate.

Ormond felt a strange mixture of relief and regret as he watched her disappear. He took a deep breath, then re-wrapped the strips in the chamois, pocketed them, and started walking the three-quarters of a mile toward the hospital.

He was still amazed. With these coins, along with those Johnson had, the collection was complete, except for the one coin they'd used to buy their way to Cuba. What would C.E.'s reaction be when his son walked in and handed him the missing gold? Ormond resolved to be neutral to anything the old man might say or do. His parents would have to deal with the insurance company.

The windfall was quickening his recovery. A great weight had been lifted from him; he was walking on a cloud. Wait until Johnson and Gunderson heard about this!

But the euphoria wore off after ten minutes, and he paused to rest, leaning on the iron picket fence that marked the entrance to the grounds of the Grant House, residence of the Ordnance Department's commanding officer. He glanced at the large archway, supported on either side by upended cannon. Two smaller cannon outside the large ones bracketed smaller pedestrian gates. The fence itself was fashioned of tapered Civil War musket barrels, fixed bayonets thrusting upward.

He ran his hands over the painted, inert ironwork, wondering how many men had been killed by musket balls fired from these barrels. "Swords into plowshares," he muttered aloud. "They make a good picket fence."

He straightened up and strode confidently away along the narrow road, at peace with himself.

Author's Note

Some historians believe the Spanish-American War was the beginning of American imperialism. Others feel the conflict was necessary to free the suppressed Cuban people from centuries of Spanish domination. If the latter view is correct, it proved to be only a brief respite.

A United States military government ruled Cuba from 1898–1902 when Tomás Estrada Palma was elected president. American troops were then withdrawn, only to return during a rebellion against the Palma government in 1906–1909.

A black uprising broke out in 1912. Then, a workers' revolt in 1917 threatened to shut down many of the American-owned sugar mills, plantations, and businesses. During both of these rebellions, American troops were sent back to Cuba to protect American property. Subsequent revolutions and dictatorships from within have kept the Cuban people subjugated into the 21st century.

In terms of casualties, the war of 1898 was a minor skirmish compared to the global horror of the Great War (in which Theodore Roosevelt lost a son). But to those directly affected, the Cuban conflict was as deadly and heart-rending as any other.

About the Author

Tim Champlin, born John Michael Champlin in Fargo, North Dakota, was graduated from Middle Tennessee State University and earned a Master's degree from Peabody College in Nashville, Tennessee. Beginning his career as an author of the Western story with *Summer of the Sioux* in 1982, the American West represents for him "a huge, ever-changing block of space and time in which an individual had more freedom than the average person has today. For those brave, and sometimes desperate souls who ventured West looking for a better life, it must have been an exciting time to be alive." Champlin has achieved a notable stature in being able to capture that time in complex, often exciting, and historically accurate fictional narratives. He is the author of two series of Western novels, one concerned with Matt Tierney who comes of age in *Summer of the Sioux* and who begins his professional career as a reporter for the Chicago *Times-Herald* covering an expeditionary force venturing into the Big Horn country and the Yellowstone, and one with Jay McGraw, a callow youth who is plunged into outlawry at the beginning of *Colt Lightning*. There are six books in the Matt Tierney series and with *Deadly Season* a fifth featuring Jay McGraw. In *The Last Campaign,* Champlin provides a compelling narrative of Geronimo's last days as a renegade leader. *Swift Thunder* is an exciting and compelling story of the Pony Express. *Wayfaring Strangers* is an extraordinary story of the California Gold Rush. In all of Champlin's stories there are always unconventional plot ingredients, striking historical details, vivid characterizations of the multitude of ethnic and cultural diversity found on the frontier, and narratives rich and original and surprising. His exuberant tapestries include lumber schooners sailing the West Coast, early-day wet-plate photography, daredevils who thrill crowds with gas balloons and the first parachutes, tong wars in San Francisco's Chinatown, Basque sheepherders, and the *Penitentes* of the Southwest, and are always highly entertaining. *Devil's Domain: Far From the Eye of God* is his next **Five Star Western**.